She had to be crazy...

Coming here alone in the middle of the night. In fact, ever since Morgan had arrived at Ben's estate a week ago, she had been doing crazy things. She hoped trusting Ben Wells wouldn't prove to be one of them.

After hearing his explanation of her father's death, she had agreed to act as Ben's liaison with Josh whatever-his-last-name-was, his private investigator. If Ben's story was accurate, only Josh's assistance stood between her and Ben and the man who stalked them. And only with Josh's help could they expose her father's killer.

Gathering her courage, Morgan knocked at the sagging door. The hoot of an owl in the lonely meadow gave her the shivers. But chills of a different, intimate sort ran down her spine when a deep masculine voice from the darkness said, "Come in."

Morgan moved forward blindly, and not only because she couldn't see. She knew even less about the mysterious Josh than she did about Ben Wells.

Dear Reader,

You've told us that stories about hidden identities are some of your favorites, so this month we're happy to bring them to you, in the all-new HIDDEN IDENTITY promotion.

Charlotte Douglas's men are indeed hidden—whether swathed in bandages or cloaked in disguise. But the sex appeal can't be denied. Find out how *Ben's Wife* learns to find the real man behind the mask.

The author of several Harlequin American Romance novels and Harlequin Intrigue books, Charlotte lives in the Tampa Bay area with her high school sweetheart, whom she married over three decades ago.

We hope you enjoy it—and all the books coming to you in HIDDEN IDENTITY.

Regards,

Debra Matteucci
Senior Editor & Editorial Coordinator
Harlequin Books
300 East 42nd Street
New York, NY 10017

Ben's Wife
Charlotte Douglas

Harlequin Books

TORONTO • NEW YORK • LONDON
AMSTERDAM • PARIS • SYDNEY • HAMBURG
STOCKHOLM • ATHENS • TOKYO • MILAN
MADRID • WARSAW • BUDAPEST • AUCKLAND

ISBN 0-373-22434-6

BEN'S WIFE

This edition published by arrangement with Harlequin Books S.A.

® and TM are trademarks of the publisher. Trademarks indicated with ® are registered in the United States Patent and Trademark Office, the Canadian Trade Marks Office and in other countries.

Printed in U.S.A.

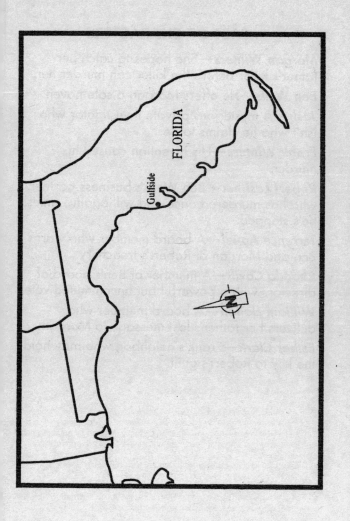

CAST OF CHARACTERS

Morgan Winters—She hopes to catch her father's killer before the killer can murder her.

Ben Wells—He offers Morgan a safe haven.

Josh—A mysterious private investigator who isn't who he claims to be.

Frank Winters—His invention caused his murder.

Robert Lashner—Ben Wells's business partner, who has murdered once and will again...unless he's stopped.

Terrence Appel—A board member who warns Ben and Morgan of Robert's treachery.

Rhonda Covill—A member of Ben's board of directors with a powerful but uncommitted vote.

William Holton—A board member who delivers her father's last message to Morgan.

Esther Clark—Frank's neighbor, who may hold the key to Robert's guilt.

Prologue

Ben Wells, president and chief executive officer of Chemco Industries, grabbed the telephone on his desk at the first ring. He'd been troubleshooting all day and didn't expect this contact to be any different. Overseeing Chemco's success had taken a heavy toll on his personal life, making social calls only a distant memory.

"You busy?" Frank Winters's genial voice was a pleasant surprise.

Ben welcomed his friend's interruption of his study of quarterly financial reports that weren't balancing. "What's up?"

"Maybe nothing."

Ben frowned at the concern in the chemist's tone. "I'm listening."

"Rob Lashner asked me to meet him in the lab at seven. Said he wants to talk about the formula."

Ben swore under his breath. Every time there was trouble lately, Robert Lashner's name popped up. It was Lashner, his partner and vice president, who had vouched for the accountant who had botched the reports on Ben's desk. And Lashner had fought Ben's and Frank's refusal to sell the formula for Frank's latest discovery.

"Is Rob still pressuring you to falsify your findings?" Ben asked.

"I don't know what part of *no* he doesn't understand. Maybe if we talk to him together—"

"Good idea." Ben glanced at his watch. "It's almost seven. I'll be right over."

Ben left his office and crossed the avenue that ran between the plant's administration building and Chemco's laboratory facility. Hurrying along the landscaped plaza toward the low, modern structure, he scanned the area for Rob Lashner. The dark street was deserted. Lashner must have reached the lab ahead of him.

Inside, as Ben headed toward the hallway that led to Frank's lab, the art deco clock above the reception desk in the lobby showed 7:00 p.m. He was halfway down the hall when the air rocked with a deafening explosion.

Like a giant hand, the concussion knocked him to the floor, punched the air from his lungs, bludgeoned his ears. When the shock wave passed, Ben dragged himself to his elbows. The blast had ripped the double lab doors off their hinges. Acrid smoke billowed from the opening.

The lab was burning!

And Frank, his best friend, the man who was like a father to him, was in there.

With his ears ringing, Ben scrambled to his feet. Groping blindly through the smoke, he activated the fire alarm on the wall, yanked an extinguisher from its bracket and plunged into the lab.

"Frank!" He could barely hear himself over the roar and crackle of the flames. "Where are you?"

Thick heat from the blaze at the far end of the room clasped around him like a sweaty fist. Gasping and choking for air, he stumbled between the counters toward the fire. The automatic sprinkler system hadn't kicked in. Had the blast disabled it?

And where was Frank?

"Frank!" He gagged on deadly smoke. "Answer me!"

Dragging the extinguisher, Ben dropped to his hands and knees and crawled toward the flames. If the volatile chemicals in the adjacent storage area ignited, the explosion would take out the whole building. Breathing from the thin stream of oxygen sandwiched between two layers of lethal fumes, he scurried forward until he struck an obstacle in the aisle.

Frank.

Instinct demanded Ben stop and help his friend, but intellect reminded him they'd both be beyond saving if the flames progressed much farther.

Ben gulped air, shoved himself to his feet and lunged at the fire. With heat singing his eyebrows, he sprayed the fire with retardant, emptying the extinguisher, praying it would be enough. Slowly, the hot orange flames flickered and died beneath the blanket of foam, leaving a shroud of dense smoke hanging throughout the lab.

By the hellish crimson glare of the emergency lights filtering through the fumes, Ben returned to Frank, slumped against a counter, his lab coat damp with blood from a wound on his forehead.

He wasn't breathing.

Ben grabbed him by the shoulders. "Dammit, Frank, don't die on me."

He eased his friend onto his back, tipped the chemist's head and cleared his windpipe, then began counting breaths and compressions for CPR.

After a couple minutes that seemed like hours, Frank coughed and stirred.

"Take it easy," Ben's smoke-scarred voice rasped. "I'm going to call an ambulance."

"No time." Frank clutched his sleeve. The older man's speech was little more than a wheeze, and Ben leaned closer to hear. "Get out. Fast."

"Don't worry. The fire's out. There's no danger—"

"Lashner. He set the explosion." Frank inhaled with tortured, sucking gasps and attempted to rise. "He wants to kill us both. For the formula."

Frank's blow to the head had made him delusional. Ben pressed Frank's shoulders to the floor. "This can wait."

"No." Frank gripped the front of Ben's shirt and pulled him closer. "You must look after Morgan. Please, take care of my daughter, Ben."

"You can look after—"

The older man's grip tightened. "Promise."

"I promise, Frank. Now, just lie back—"

"No time. Two explosions."

"Two?"

"Lashner set the first one to bring you running. Didn't know I'd already called you."

So Lashner really did intend to kill him. Fury cleared Ben's mind and speeded his actions. From beneath a counter, he dragged out a blanket used to smother lab fires. After slinging Frank in a fireman's carry, he tossed the blanket over both of them and raced down the aisle between the counters. His lungs burned from smoke and chemical fumes, and the weight of Frank's inert body racked his shoulders, shooting waves of agony through his muscles.

If he could just get them outside, they'd be safe. Then together they'd see that Lashner paid for his treachery.

"Take care of Morgan, Ben." Frank's ebbing voice wheezed against his ear.

Tears from smoke, anger and grief coursed down Ben's cheeks. "I'll get you out of here, buddy, so you can take care of her yourself. Everything's going to be all right."

The detonation of the second blast drowned his words, and a wall of flame seared him with white-hot agony. He stumbled through the lab entrance and forced his buckling knees and bursting lungs to carry him, with Frank still over his shoulders, up the hall. In the lobby, he collapsed into the hands of two firemen rushing in the front door.

He was conscious only of someone lifting Frank from his shoulders before the lobby floor came up to meet him. The cool, hard ceramic tiles smacked his cheek, and the world turned black as smoke.

Chapter One

"You're a lucky woman, Miss Winters."

"Lucky?" Morgan Winters said with stunned surprise. "You've got to be kidding."

"You have to look on the bright side." The young emergency room clerk with the cheerleader smile returned Morgan's insurance card. "Without your car's side air bags, you would have been killed."

"That's what the police said." Morgan forced a shaky smile, but she didn't feel lucky. Not after losing her father. She rubbed her aching shoulder, then tucked her card into her wallet. "Would you call me a cab, please?"

"Sure." The clerk reach for the phone on the admittance desk. Suddenly her grin faded. "Hey, you look pretty wobbly. You'd better sit down."

Morgan didn't argue. On unstable legs, she turned toward a row of vinyl-covered chairs, collapsed onto a seat and rested her throbbing head against the wall.

She was hundreds of miles from home in the unfamiliar city of Gulfside, Florida, and had never felt so totally alone. Closing her eyes, she tried to recall details of her father's funeral, the minister's brief eulogy, the blur of strange faces.

"Miss Winters?" The clerk's summons jolted Morgan from her grief.

Maybe her cab had arrived.

Morgan peered through the double glass doors at the emergency room entrance. Except for an idling ambulance, the driveway was deserted. She turned back to the clerk.

"Telephone for you." The clerk waved the receiver and motioned her toward the desk.

Still dazed from the morning's funeral and subsequent hit-and-run collision, Morgan took the call.

"Miss Winters," a strangely muffled voice said, "this is Ben Wells."

She needed a few seconds to identify the vaguely familiar name. Benjamin Wells was president and CEO of Chemco Industries where her father had worked as head chemist, where he had died in the laboratory fire. According to police, Wells had nearly lost his own life trying to rescue her father.

"Mr. Wells—"

"There's no time for talk." His peculiar wheezing voice vibrated in her ear. "Just listen. Your father's death was no accident."

"What?"

"Your father was murdered."

Light-headed, she felt the room begin to spin. "But—"

"And the hit-and-run driver at the cemetery today tried to kill you, too. He almost succeeded."

"How—"

"I can't explain now, but you're in great danger.

My injuries prevent my coming to you, but if you'll take a cab to my house—''

"How do I know you *are* Ben Wells?" She struggled to understand through the throbbing in her head. "I've never met you."

"You trust your father's secretary. Call Brenda Jernigan and ask for my home address. She'll vouch for me."

The room rotated again. "I don't know—"

Uncertainty crippled her. Ben Wells had been her father's friend. Yet, for all she knew, the man could be as paranoid as he was rich.

But if he *was* right about her father's death and her accident…

"Hurry," the wheezing voice commanded. "Every minute you waste places you in greater danger."

The line went dead.

MORGAN STUMBLED through the midnight darkness along an unfamiliar path Ben Wells had said would lead her to an isolated cottage on the bay.

The papery rustle of palms accompanied her steps, and the fragrance of flowers and salt air filled the gentle breeze. In the distance at the mouth of the secluded bay, the Gulf of Mexico, silvered by the rising moon, stretched toward the horizon. Under different circumstances, the vista would seem a postcard-perfect Florida scene.

She had to be crazy, coming here alone in the middle of the night. In fact, ever since she first arrived at Ben's estate a week ago, she had been doing crazy things. She hoped trusting Ben Wells wouldn't prove one of them.

After hearing his explanation of her father's death, she had agreed to act as Ben's liaison with Josh, his private investigator. If Ben's story was accurate, only Josh's assistance stood between her and Ben and the man who stalked them. And only with Josh's help could they expose her father's killer.

With reluctance, she climbed the rickety steps to the porch and stepped into the deep shadows of tangled Virginia creeper that overran the house. Maybe nobody would be home. Then she could flee to the safety of Ben's mansion once more. Gathering her courage, she knocked at the sagging door, and powdery aging paint dusted her knuckles.

The splash of distant surf broke the stillness, and at the mournful hoot of an owl, she shivered despite the warm night air. Josh whatever-his-last-name-was was certainly taking his own sweet time.

She brushed oxidized paint from her fingers, rapped again and heard the knock reverberate through the empty rooms. No one responded, and she turned to leave.

The high-pitched creak of door hinges stopped her cold. Peering past the half-open door, she could see nothing but inky blackness.

"Josh?" she said with a waver of hesitation.

"Who are you?"

At the voice's deep richness, tinged with a hint of menace, a chill radiated through her. "It's Morgan. Ben Wells sent me. He said you were expecting me."

The door shrieked as it opened wider. Only a thin

stream of moonlight, spilling through an uncurtained window in a room at the far end of the hall, was visible.

"Come in before someone spots you." The disembodied voice floated eerily on the night air. "And watch your step. I won't turn on a light until I'm certain you weren't followed."

Treading with caution, she entered the dark hallway. The door swung shut behind her, and she jumped as a dead bolt slammed home. With effort, she willed her tightened muscles to relax.

Ben wouldn't have sent her if it wasn't safe.

Would he?

A strong hand grasped her elbow, and she flinched and muffled a squeal of surprise.

"Sorry to startle you—" regret tinged his voice "—but if I don't guide you, you'll trip over something."

With her sight restricted, Morgan's other senses shifted into high gear. Josh's touch, solid evidence he was more than just a voice, warmed her elbow, and he loomed tall and powerful beside her in the darkness. Inside the shuttered cottage, the subtle aroma of spicy soap, a hint of leather and the tangy scent of the sea floated on the still air.

She moved forward blindly, and not only because she couldn't see. She knew even less about the mysterious Josh than she did about Ben Wells.

Josh led her into a room awash with pale moon glow and steered her to a chair. Before she could glimpse his face, he retreated into the shadows.

"Comfortable?" he asked.

Amazingly, she was. The roomy armchair embraced her, and she sniffed a lingering mélange of lemon oil, beeswax and soap. She had expected a dirty, deserted house, draped in cobwebs and smothered with dust, but the room smelled fresh, as if just cleaned.

From Josh's corner came a twisting sound, a splashing of liquid and the aroma of freshly brewed coffee.

"This will keep us awake," he said, "while you tell me what's going on."

As he handed her a steaming cup, weak moonlight silhouetted the squareness of his jaw and a profile like a Greek statue. Standing over her, Josh appeared both dangerous and enigmatic. That Ben had refused to divulge Josh's last name only added to the private investigator's mystery.

Morgan sipped the hot liquid, thankful for its warmth. "I'm not sure how to begin."

"Explain," his velvet voice directed, "how you became Ben Wells's ally."

"My father is—was chief chemist for Chemco Industries. He died in last week's fire."

"I'm sorry." His voice rang with sympathy. "Frank was a good man. And a good friend. I've been away, so I don't know details of the accident."

So Josh had been her father's friend. That fact eased her shivering, until she realized her father had never mentioned anyone named Josh. She shook off her misgivings. Regrettably, she had spent so little time with her dad, she knew almost nothing about his personal life.

"Will you answer a question?" she asked.

"If I can."

"Why all this cloak-and-dagger business, midnight meetings, concealed identities?"

He crossed to a window and peered out, checking the path, the only approach to the cottage. Apparently satisfied for the moment that no one had followed her, he resumed his seat in the shadows. The chair springs creaked, another indication of his commanding size.

"I've conducted investigations for Ben for years," he said, "and his partner and employees at the plant know me. Ben wants to keep this inquiry secret, so I'll stay out of sight. Even better, let everyone believe I'm still out of town."

The sensible explanation lessened her anxiety. "Ben said I'm to tell you everything, hold nothing back."

"Start with the accident at Chemco," he prodded gently, as if aware of the pain the subject caused.

"Ben says it wasn't an accident."

Stillness settled on the room. Outside, the sea breeze strengthened, rustling the creeping vines that blanketed the house and scraping branches of Australian pine against the windows. A cloud drifted across the moon, deepening the darkness.

"What makes Ben think the fire wasn't an accident?" Josh's level voice was void of emotion.

"Robert Lashner."

"Ben's partner?"

She nodded, then realized he couldn't see her response. "Yes."

"How is Lashner involved in this?"

"Robert Lashner was ecstatic about my father's

most recent discovery. Shortly before he died, Dad invented a compound that can replace fossil fuels.''

Josh emitted a low whistle of surprise. "Such a find would virtually eliminate the need for gasoline.''

Morgan remembered her father's excited phone call the evening of his discovery. It was the last time she'd spoken with him. "Not only would the inexpensive compound end the drain on natural resources, it could also change the balance of economic and political power in the world. Access to oil would no longer be a trump card.''

"Pretty potent stuff.''

"*Too* potent. According to Ben, after his initial breakthrough, my father made an additional finding. The compound exhibits extreme instability and volatility under certain circumstances.''

"What circumstances?''

The strangeness of this midnight meeting with a man she had yet to view face-to-face unsettled her, but, determined to keep her promise to act as Ben's emissary, she resisted an overpowering compulsion to bolt out the door.

"What makes the compound unsafe?'' Josh asked again.

She grasped the arms of her chair and concentrated on her mission. "Dad couldn't pinpoint which factors caused the instability. They fluctuated from one experiment to another. He explained to Ben that the product was unsafe and therefore worthless.''

"Frank couldn't correct the formula?''

"Ben said no matter what adjustments Dad made, he couldn't guarantee the product's stability. Under test situations, it exploded at least eight percent of the time. Dad intended to recommend that the board of directors reject the product."

She stared into the darkness, accustomed now to the gloom. Moonlight outlined Josh's broad shoulders, the strong column of his neck, long legs stretched out before him and crossed casually at the ankles, and the bulk of what appeared to be a holstered gun at his hip. A rock-solid man, the type she would want on her side if trouble came. His aura of strength piqued her imagination and agitated her overstimulated senses. She craved an extended look at him in good light.

"So your father was going to nix the compound," he said. "Go on."

The darkness concealed her flush of embarrassment at being caught musing again.

"The night of the fire," she said, "Ben was working late. He received a call from my father, asking him to meet him at the lab. By the time Ben arrived, the lab was engulfed in flames. Ben grabbed a fire extinguisher and fought his way through to Dad."

Sorrow obstructed her voice, and she swallowed hard in order to continue. "Dad wasn't breathing, so Ben performed CPR. My father revived only long enough to warn Ben that Lashner had set the fire in an attempt to kill them both."

"Why would Lashner want to kill his own partner and his best chemist?"

"So he could convince the board to sell the compound's formula, without opposition from Dad or Ben, and reap the profits."

In telling the story, Morgan confronted the harsh reality of her father's death for the first time. Her dad was gone. She would never see his smile, hear him laugh or feel his hugs again. Tears she had been unable to shed at the funeral ran down her cheeks, and in spite of her effort to suppress them, sobs racked her.

"I'm sorry," she mumbled through her weeping, "I didn't mean to—"

"Go ahead and cry." His tenderness intensified her tears. "Let it all out. You'll feel better."

She ached for the reassuring heat of flesh and blood, a living barrier against the unbearable desolation and pain. The loss of her father, her only living relative, had left her completely alone.

As if recognizing her need, Josh rose from his chair, lifted her against the warm hardness of his chest and stroked her hair. She yielded to the solace of his embrace and, as her crying eased, noted the paradox of his gentle response and tough demeanor.

Confronting a paradox of her own, she broke away from his seductive closeness while longing to remain in the comfort of his arms. She choked back a hysterical laugh. Grief had undoubtedly made her crazy.

"Feeling better?" he asked.

Afraid to trust her voice, she nodded.

He reached into his pocket for a handkerchief and handed it to her. Moonlight glittered in his dark eyes.

"Blow."

She did as he said, then returned to her chair and focused on her assignment to distract herself from the magnetism of his looming closeness.

Ben had been specific in his instructions, even though she'd seen little of him during the week she'd spent in his home. Confined to a wheelchair, his

burns swathed in bandages that covered his face and
hands, he had slept most of the week. Dark glasses
shielded his injured eyes. Because of his damaged
lungs, he required an oxygen mask and found talking
exhausting. In his attempt to save her father, he had
paid a terrible price.

Painstakingly, over a period of days, a few minutes
at a time, Ben had provided bits and pieces of the
story she now related to Josh.

"Ben," she said, "was terribly injured in the
blaze. That's why your help is so important to him."

"Has he gone to the police with his suspicions?"
Josh's voice displayed none of the inner turmoil he
made her feel. The man's ability to squelch emotion
must make him a cool and effective investigator.

"Without proof? Lashner knew how to stage a
chemical mishap. According to the arson investigators, the physical evidence supports an accidental explosion and fire. Ben, through Dad's dying declaration, knows better. That's why he needs you. And
me."

He retreated to his chair. "Don't tell me you're an
investigator, too."

"No." The idea made her smile. "But as Frank
Winters's daughter, I can search dad's home and office and question his associates without raising suspicions."

"What about Ben? If Lashner really wants him
dead, he won't stop now."

Her heart hammered at the possibility. Impressed
by Ben's courage and selflessness, she had developed
a deep affection for her father's friend. "Ben has had
reports circulated that his injuries are life-threatening

and he's not expected to live. He figures Lashner will wait to see if he dies before taking the trouble to kill him."

"Isn't that risky?"

"I tried to convince him to leave the country until you can discover the proof he needs, but he refuses. He says between his state-of-the-art security system and Harper's presence, he's perfectly safe at home."

Harper, Ben's enormous and silent valet, had driven her to this rendezvous and waited for her now at the head of the path.

"Do you believe Ben's on the level?" Josh asked.

The question stunned and angered her. "He was my father's best friend, as well as his boss. And from the time I've spent with him, I'd swear to his integrity. But why am I telling you this? You know him better than I do."

"Just checking," he said with a smile in his voice. "I need to know where your loyalties lie."

"*My* loyalties!" Indignation forced her to her feet. "You can't believe I'd come to this godforsaken place in the middle of the night to confer with a complete stranger if I didn't intend to help Ben?"

He strode across the room, grasped her by the shoulders and thrust his face close to hers. Her mutinous senses leaped at his touch. "Ben believed Lashner, his mentor and partner, was loyal. That trust almost got him killed."

He sounded tough, but she could sense the compassion beneath his hard-boiled veneer. Unafraid, she tilted her face toward his. "I'm not Lashner."

"No." His grasp eased, and a peculiar softness

filled his voice. "But be careful whom you trust. Your life could depend on it."

"Let's get one thing straight." She twisted from his grasp before she succumbed to her desire to have him hold her again. "Lashner killed my father. I'll do anything to see that he's punished."

"Anything?"

"Anything that doesn't harm someone else in the process." She laid her hand on his forearm, bridging the gap she'd forced between them. Her blood warmed with the heat rising from the corded muscles beneath her fingers.

"We can't catch Lashner if we don't work together," she said in a conciliatory tone, "and we can't work together if you won't trust me."

He covered her hand with his, and his grip consoled her. The moment lengthened, vibrating in the silence of the lightless room, and she longed to see his face.

"I have to trust you." A curious huskiness roughened his tone. "And you mustn't forget that Ben's life, and mine, hinge on that trust."

She staggered, overwrought with grief and the weariness of countless sleepless nights. Her father's untimely death, her car crash, Ben's strange revelations during the past week, and now this remarkable encounter with a stranger who inexplicably roused her senses all bore down on her.

She retreated to her chair and swallowed the last of her coffee. Disregarding her frayed nerves, she concentrated on her purpose. Ben had urged her to keep nothing from Josh.

"There's something else you need to know," she said.

"What's that?"

"My father took part of his pension and all his bonuses from Chemco Industries in stock. His will leaves everything to me."

"How much stock are you talking about?"

"Enough to swing a majority of votes to either Ben or Lashner."

"So if Lashner purchased your stock, he'd have the clout to order Chemco to sell the compound's formula?"

The man was quick. No wonder Ben had such confidence in him. "Exactly. And *without* my votes, Ben won't have enough to stop him."

Silence reigned momentarily in Josh's corner of the room. "You could make yourself a bundle by selling to the highest bidder."

She stiffened at the insult. "Lashner murdered my father! Besides, he knows I'll honor my father's wishes to keep the compound off the market." She exhaled a deep breath. "That's why Lashner tried to kill me, too."

"When?" His simple question lacked surprise. Maybe Ben had told him of the attempt on her life. Or maybe Josh had already guessed what Lashner's reaction would be.

"Immediately after my father's funeral, my car was broadsided by a hit-and-run driver. Except for side air bags, I'd be dead now. Ben believes Lashner was behind the attempt."

Josh cleared his throat. "I don't mean to sound

indelicate, but what would have happened to your stock if your collision had been fatal?''

''It would have been tied up in probate for a year or more, long enough for Lashner to garner enough votes from the other directors to override Ben's objections to selling the compound's formula.''

''So you've sold your stock to Ben?''

''No, he didn't ask to buy it. But I've guaranteed that Lashner can't tie it up if anything happens to me.''

''How?'' This time, he sounded astonished.

''Please, don't mention this to Ben.''

''Why not?''

''I haven't told him yet.'' She hesitated. Could she trust Josh? According to Ben, she had no choice. ''Today I instructed my lawyer to place the stock in an irrevocable living trust for my husband.''

''Husband? You're married?''

''I assumed Ben told you,'' she said with feigned nonchalance. ''I married him yesterday.''

Chapter Two

"Everything's clear. Looks like no one followed you."

Josh surveyed the moonlit grounds through the exposed window, then pulled the shade and drew the curtains. After shielding the other windows, he switched on a small lamp on the table beside Morgan.

Because his life depended on her loyalty and truthfulness, he had to observe her face. Only the most practiced liars could hide their deception from a trained observer. Frank Winters had been his friend and had always spoken highly of his daughter, but parental love was sometimes blind. Josh needed to confirm his gut feeling that Morgan could be trusted.

For a clearer view of her responses, he dragged a straight chair opposite her and straddled it, slowly, deliberately, leaning his forearm on the ladder back.

The roomy armchair engulfed her slender body, clad in a crisp white blouse, fitted jeans and sneakers. The contrast of her small frame to the huge chair emphasized her vulnerability and activated a deep, empathetic response. He forced the tender feelings away. Succumbing to sentiment could impair his instincts and get him killed.

Her, too, if she was on the level.

Morgan's eyes, the deep, tranquil blue of an October sky and wide with fright, focused on him with fierce intensity. Her apprehension, at least, was honest. Someone had murdered her father and was now after her. Only a fool would experience no fear in those circumstances.

The woman's succinct questions and articulate explanations proved she was no fool.

He assessed her closely in the lamplight. With shoulder-length hair the color of champagne, an oval face and a roses-and-cream complexion marred only by a tiny, almost-healed scratch above her left eye, Morgan Winters resembled a Renaissance painting of an angel come to life.

He grimaced at the irony. Whether her personality matched her angelic exterior, only time would tell.

Heat, kindled by her beauty, flared deep in his groin, producing a definitely unangelic response. Recalling Frank Winters's horrible death cooled his desire. He couldn't afford distractions.

"You married Ben *yesterday?*" He pressed her to gauge her reactions. "Kind of sudden, wasn't it? I mean, he's never mentioned you before."

Her shoulders stiffened in defense. "We met the day of my father's funeral."

He lifted his brows and whistled. "You *are* a fast worker."

Blue flames danced in her eyes. "It's not what you think."

"That you're an opportunist? That Ben Wells is a

very wealthy man?'' With reluctance, he pushed his attack, in spite of her cringing at his words. ''That, if he doesn't die from his current injuries, they could drastically shorten his life, making his widow a very wealthy woman?''

''Marrying me was *Ben's* idea.''

''Yeah, right. What does Wells have to gain from marrying you?''

An enchanting shade of pink crept from the open neckline of her shirt to her hairline. ''We've agreed our marriage is in name only.''

''A marriage of convenience? Without connubial bliss?''

Her blush deepened, causing him well-deserved discomfort at his frank questions.

But he couldn't stop now. He had to determine exactly where she stood. ''So what's in it for Ben?''

''My stock's voting rights.''

''You said he didn't ask to buy your stock.''

She shook her head, and a strand of golden hair tumbled across her forehead and over one eye. He resisted the urge to brush it back.

Combing her hair off her face with her fingers, she inclined her chin and glared at him. ''According to my father's will, I couldn't exercise my voting privileges, or sell my stock, until after I was married.''

''I didn't know Frank was so old-fashioned.''

''The stock restrictions were his way of trying to protect me.''

''So by marrying you,'' he said, ''Ben enables you to vote, hopefully in his favor.''

''I've already told you I would vote with Ben,'' she said through gritted teeth.

He pushed her further. "What do you gain from this farce of a marriage, besides Ben's fortune?"

"Ben's fortune is safe. I signed a prenuptial agreement." She averted her eyes, and confusion fluttered briefly across her delicate features before she faced him again. "You don't trust me. Why?"

Josh silently tallied the reasons. He knew almost nothing about Morgan except what her father had told him. Regardless of her spur-of-the-moment marriage, Morgan owed no loyalty to Ben Wells. If Lashner offered to buy her votes and dangled big bucks and a promise of posthumous fame for Frank Winters for discovering the compound, Josh couldn't be sure how she'd react. Especially if Lashner's deal included sparing her life. However, Josh wasn't about to give her any ideas by sharing his misgivings.

"You have to earn trust," he said, "and I don't know enough about you yet for that."

"I'd say we're even in the trust department. With one exception."

"What's that?"

"I *want* to trust you. For the same reason I married Ben Wells."

"Why did you marry Ben?"

"To help catch my father's k-killer." Although earnestness sparked in her cobalt eyes, her voice faltered.

"A noble goal," he said with a hint of skepticism. She dropped her gaze, and he suspected she was holding something back. "Any other reasons?"

She raised her head and met his stare straight on. "Ben promised to protect me from Lashner and his associates."

"*Assassins* is a better word."

"Assassins?" she whispered, as if afraid of the word. Her hands trembled slightly before she clasped them motionless on her knees, and color drained from her face.

Josh silently cursed the clumsiness of his interrogation. He had only wanted to shock her into telling all, but he'd succeeded in scaring her to death. He tamped down the urge to hold her, to ease her fears.

"You don't think Lashner would soil his own hands, do you?" he asked. "He hires out his dirty work."

"Like the driver who hit my car?" She leaned against the chair back and closed her eyes. The roses had vanished from her cheeks, and her golden lashes brushed mauve shadows, signs of her exhaustion.

"When's the last time you had a good night's sleep?" He failed to repress the tenderness in his voice.

She opened her eyes and struggled upright. "The night before my father died. But I'm fine."

"You don't look fine. You look ready to collapse."

"I'm tougher than I look. Let's get on with it."

"It?"

"Ben said you have a plan to expose Lashner."

Josh nodded. "I do, but you're not going to like it."

"I don't like any of this, particularly your tactless questions." She rubbed her eyes with her fists in an obvious effort to stay alert. "Even my ordinary and uneventful life back home in Memphis is preferable to being cross-examined like a criminal. It's Lashner you should be interrogating.''

"You could go home, away from Lashner," he said, testing her resolve, yet knowing he couldn't allow her to leave. "Forget any of this ever happened."

Fists still clenched, she dropped her hands to her lap. "*Forget* someone murdered my father? How cold-blooded do you think I am?"

Cold-blooded enough to marry a man she barely knew. "You'll have to be ruthless for the scheme I have in mind."

Her head snapped up, and outrage blazed in her weary eyes. "I want justice, not revenge. If Lashner is punished, the courts must do it."

He grinned at her misinterpretation. "I'm not a hit man, if that's what you're thinking."

"Then what did you mean by *ruthless?*" She narrowed her eyes, creating a furrow in her forehead.

Her range of expressions fascinated him, and with difficulty he concentrated on her question.

"To get the goods on Lashner, you'll have to take chances."

"What kind of chances?"

He assessed Morgan's beguiling mixture of strength and vulnerability, of fear and determination, and what had previously seemed a good strategy appeared suddenly less attractive. "You'll have to provide a visible target for his goons."

She leaped to her feet, scooted past his chair and backed toward the door. "You want to use *me* as bait? You're out of your mind."

He hoisted himself from his chair and, in two long

strides, faced her. The top of her head reached only to his chin, making her seem more delicate than ever. He toughened himself against her fragility. "If we can catch one of Lashner's hired guns and have him charged with attempted murder, maybe he'll give us Lashner in a plea bargain."

"You're forgetting one minor detail." Her sarcasm pummeled him. "What if Lashner's assassin kills me *before* you catch him?"

"I won't let that happen."

Morgan Winters was an extremely desirable woman, and her righteous anger heightened her appeal. He clasped his hands behind his back to keep from touching her.

"For a man so slow to trust, you have some nerve asking me to put my life in your hands."

Before he could stop her, she marched out of the room and down the hall. The cottage walls shook as the front door slammed behind her.

Realizing pursuit was futile, he slumped into the easy chair, still warm from Morgan's body and fragrant with her jasmine perfume.

She hadn't given him a chance to explain that she was already Lashner's target, whether she agreed to the plan or not.

To keep her alive, Ben Wells would have to convince her to cooperate.

BEN SLOUCHED in his motorized wheelchair and watched the sun dip toward the horizon beyond the glass walls of his living room. Harper had driven Morgan home at three o'clock this morning, and she had been asleep ever since. Josh had confirmed her loyalty but had failed to enlist her help.

It was left to Ben to persuade her.

His bandages abraded his skin, and his injuries skewered him with white-hot agony. He couldn't take pain pills. He needed a clear head to deal with Morgan.

When he closed his eyes behind his dark glasses, Frank Winters's face, seared with burns, loomed in his memory.

"Take care of my girl, Ben," the dying man had begged. "Don't let Lashner hurt her."

He had promised Frank through his tears. The chemist had been his best friend, but Ben was indebted to Frank for much more than the affection they'd shared. Winters's genius had been responsible for much of Chemco's prosperity, and before he died, Frank had forewarned Ben of Lashner's treachery.

Morgan had expressed her gratitude for Ben's attempt to save her father, but she didn't know the whole story. Only Frank's alerting Ben to a second explosion had enabled Ben to escape. He had exchanged the weight of his dead friend, carried across his shoulders out of the burning lab, for his obligation to keep Morgan safe.

Since learning about the hit-and-run driver who had almost killed her, he had gone without sleep, searching for a plan to expose Lashner's crimes without risking Morgan.

So far, no luck.

Lashner had already tried to kill her once. If he'd been interested only in acquiring her stock, he would have made an offer first. If she had accepted, he could have avoided the capital offense.

No, from the beginning, Lashner had resorted to murder to insure Morgan's silence. Besides Lashner, she and Ben were the only two alive who knew about the instability of Frank's amazing discovery. With both of them dead, Lashner would have a clear field to sell Frank's formula to the highest bidder and leave the country with his profits before the compound's flaw was discovered. Totally without conscience, Lashner wouldn't let the possibility that the product might kill people hinder his plans.

Ben gripped the wheelchair arms until his hands hurt. He might be confined to this contraption now, but he still had a few tricks up his sleeves. Lashner didn't know Frank had warned Ben or that Ben had married Morgan. If Ben's luck held, he would have more than a few surprises for his traitorous partner.

At the sound of approaching footsteps, he flipped the toggle control and swiveled his chair toward the doorway.

Mrs. Denny, his housekeeper, waited on the threshold. "Dinner will be served soon, sir. Shall I awaken Mrs. Wells?"

Ben smiled beneath his oxygen mask. Had she been born male, Mrs. Denny, with her aristocratic British accent and snooty bearing, would have made an exceptionally proper butler. "Yes, thank—"

"That won't be necessary." Morgan walked past the housekeeper into the room.

The older woman raised her eyebrows at the suitcase in Morgan's hand, then composed her features quickly before slipping quietly away.

Dread settled over Ben at the determination on his wife's face. "Going somewhere?"

She set down the luggage with a thud and swung the tote bag from her shoulder to the floor. "I'm going home. My plane leaves in two hours."

"But this is your home—"

"We can quit playing 'let's pretend.'" More elegant in jeans and a blazer than other women would be in Chanel suits, she straightened her shoulders and removed a paper from her pocket. "Here's the proxy for my stock. As soon as you've prevented Lashner from selling the formula, you can have our marriage annulled."

She advanced across the room and laid the paper on the blanket across his lap.

He ignored it, and it fluttered to the floor. "Did Josh frighten you that much?"

When she met his gaze, he detected uncertainty beneath her outward assurance.

"You promised," she said with a hitch in her voice, "to protect me from Lashner. According to Josh, I've been nominated sacrificial lamb."

She implied Ben had let her down, and the accusation hurt. "Whether you go or stay, Lashner will try to kill you."

"He'll forget about me if I go home to Memphis and keep my nose out of his business."

"If I believed that, I would have booked your flight myself, right after the hit-and-run." Panic spiraled in his gut. He'd promised Frank to look after her. How could he protect her if she was more than seven hundred miles away?

"This is between you and Lashner now," she said.

"What happened to your desire to see Lashner punished for your father's death?"

"I have a greater desire to stay alive." Her wistful, apologetic smile enhanced her beauty.

He had to keep her talking until he could convince her to stay. If only he could spring from this blasted chair and hold her—but that would frighten her more than she already was. Her poise didn't hide the anxiety in her eyes. "Sit down. Let's talk about this. I'm stronger today and can answer more of your questions."

She stooped, retrieved the proxy and laid it on the table beside him. "Josh gave me all the answers I need."

He couldn't lie and promise she'd suffer no harm if she stayed. "You'll be safer here with Josh and Harper to protect you. If you go back to Memphis, Lashner will come after you. You'll be alone—"

"Lashner doesn't want me. You control my vote. That's all he's interested in."

He clenched his fists, and the agony of his injuries seared him. He had to break through her denial. "Morgan, please—"

"Take care of yourself, Ben. Get well and stay safe." She reached out as if to take his hand, but stopped short of touching his bandages. "Thank you for all you've done, for all you tried to do."

The determination in her eyes confirmed further argument was pointless. She had convinced herself Lashner would spare her if she returned home. Nothing could break through her illogical refusal to face dangerous reality.

"I'll ring for Harper. He'll drive you to the airport," he said.

"I've already called a cab." The feathery touch of her fingers brushed the gauze that covered his face. "Goodbye, Ben."

Mrs. Denny stepped into the room. "Your cab is here, Mrs. Wells."

Without a backward glance, Morgan picked up her luggage and disappeared into the foyer, leaving only a trace of jasmine perfume behind.

Ben wheeled to his desk and depressed the button on his intercom. "Harper, get in here. Fast. We have a problem."

THROUGH THE CAB'S rear window, Morgan watched the wrought-iron gates of Ben's estate swing shut in the taillights' red glow and battled an onslaught of giddiness.

Everything had happened so fast. Her father's death, the attempt on her life, Ben's accusations against Lashner, followed by his startling proposal of marriage. The escalating momentum of events had sent her spinning.

The knockout blow had been her clandestine meeting with no-last-name Josh. Handsome. Mysterious. And deadly. His crazy scheme to nail Lashner would have gotten her killed.

For a few brief days after the funeral, she believed she had found a safe haven from Lashner in Ben Wells's waterfront estate—until her meeting with Josh proved her sanctuary a sham. She'd been stunned to learn her husband expected her to endanger herself to entrap his partner. And the inscrutable

Josh had seemed eager to assist in placing her life on the line.

A disturbing idea niggled in the back of her mind. What if it wasn't Lashner who had tried to kill her? What if Ben had hired Josh to stage the car crash in an effort to solicit her help? After all, what did she know about Ben?

Your father loved and respected him, and you trust him. More than any other man you've ever met, her conscience argued, pricking her for her doubts.

She reclined against the scratchy seat of the musty cab and tried, without much luck, to think straight. Even after twelve hours of uninterrupted slumber, her mind and body hadn't rebounded from sleep deprivation. Her movements were as sluggish as a diver's in a deep-sea suit. Her mind functioned with even less alacrity.

Regret joined the muddle in her mind. She didn't love Ben Wells. Their marriage was a temporary arrangement, but by a remote chance, she might have built a permanent life with him, caring for the invalid in return for protection and companionship. He was only about ten years her senior, and eventually they might have found something in common besides Lashner's treachery.

Dream on, girl. Lack of sleep has made you crazy.

Okay, so maybe it wouldn't have happened, but it hadn't hurt to dream. Not if her instincts were right about Ben.

One thing was certain. A marriage to Ben was more realistic than a working partnership with Josh. His forceful presence, his intoxicating scent, the contour of his profile and his velvet-smooth voice had sent hormones reeling through her bloodstream like drunken sailors. In the lamplight, his extraordinary looks, beautiful in a rugged way, had stolen her breath, while a saner part of her noted the secrets hidden in his eyes.

She had to be out of her mind.

She'd allowed her emotions to be roused by a man who'd regarded her only as a lure for a killer. So much for instinct, when it made her crave a man who obviously had ice water running through his veins.

No, she'd grown too old at twenty-eight to believe the man of her dreams would ever materialize. Soon she'd be back in Memphis, her hasty pseudomarriage annulled, and prospects for a home, family and children about as substantial as smoke on a windy day.

As the cab traveled across the bay causeway toward Tampa International Airport, she gazed with bleary vision at the swath of silver moonlight reflecting off the smooth waters. Ben had her proxy and, with it, enough votes to stop the formula's sale. He no longer needed her, but the fact gave her no comfort. She couldn't shake the ridiculous notion that, by leaving Ben, she had turned her back on her one true chance for happiness.

Going home was the right thing to do, wasn't it?

Her head ached with the same uncertainty and insecurity that had prevented her from taking chances all her life, in everything from jobs to relationships.

For a fleeting instant, she considered ordering the driver to turn back. So what if she gambled her life to trap Lashner? She would never truly live, or love, until she was willing to take risks.

But try as she would, she couldn't force herself to

face the challenge. Her innate anxiety restrained her from seizing her opportunity, and her urge to run back to Ben vanished as quickly as it came.

Forgive me, Daddy, for lacking the courage to catch your killer. I guess I wasn't meant to be a hero.

She shifted her thoughts to Memphis, and by the time the cab arrived at the drop-off for departing flights, she had almost convinced herself she was looking forward to her one-bedroom apartment and her humdrum job in accounting at Myers Department Store.

A friendly skycap opened the cab door and offered to take her luggage, but she declined. Flinging her tote bag over her shoulder, she gripped her suitcase and edged her way through the milling crowd of tourists toward the reservation desk.

Once she had picked up her ticket and checked her luggage, she wandered among the shops along the concourse, killing time until boarding.

As she scrutinized the jewelry case in the Disney shop, the skin on the back of her neck prickled with the uneasy feeling that someone was watching. She whirled around, but the few customers in the store were concentrating on the souvenir merchandise.

At the nearest snack bar, she ordered a cup of cappuccino, then meandered toward the newsstand, unable to shake the impression someone was trailing her. Each time she looked back or caught a reflection in a display glass, no one appeared to be paying her the slightest attention.

Nerves, she assured herself, the result of grief, her accident, too little sleep and too much caffeine. After a day's rest back home in Memphis, she'd be fine.

She finished her coffee, tossed her plastic cup into a trash container and entered the newsstand. Pausing before a rack of paperbacks, she studied the covers in search of a riveting fantasy to lose her troubles in for a few hours.

She flinched when something sharp pricked between her shoulder blades.

"Make a noise or any sudden moves, and I plunge this knife straight into your heart."

The low, menacing voice alone would have frightened her, but with the accompanying blade pressed against her blazer, Morgan fought to keep her knees from giving way. Her mouth turned cottony, and fear squeezed the air from her lungs.

Her panicked gaze swept the crowded shop, but no one, not even the tall, red-bearded tourist closest to her, noticed her or the man pressed against her back. If she screamed, her assailant could kill her in an instant.

"Just do as I say," the raspy voice directed. He grabbed her arm and twisted it behind her. "Head toward the elevator. Press the up button. And don't try anything funny."

Funny? She throttled an illogical urge to laugh, fearful she'd succumb to hysterics and precipitate her sudden death. On rubbery legs and with pain stabbing her shoulder from her contorted arm, she shuffled toward the bank of elevators opposite the shops. The crowd had disappeared here, leaving no one to help, even if she dared scream.

"For eight stinking days I've been watching this airport for you," her captor muttered in her ear, "and I *hate* airports."

Her heart battered against her breastbone. The man was crazy with anger. She could hear it in his voice, feel it in the sadistic wrench of her arm.

"I'm gonna make you pay for inconveniencing me," he said in a fierce whisper. "We're going to the parking garage roof, and I'm going to push you over the side. It's a long way to the bottom."

His low, hideous laugh hurt her ears.

"You're insane," she said with more boldness than she felt. "No one will believe—"

"That Morgan Winters—" he pressed the knife deeper into the back of her blazer "—despondent over her father's accident, leaped to her death?"

She inhaled deeply to staunch the thunder of blood in her ears. Maybe she should pretend to faint—

Too quickly, the up elevator arrived.

As the doors opened with a pneumatic hiss, her assailant shoved her into the empty car. From the corner of her eye, she watched his fist strike the "close door" button. Too late she realized entering the elevator had been a fatal mistake. She swiveled, ready to burst back onto the concourse through the rapidly narrowing opening, but the red-bearded man from the newsstand stepped into the breach, thrust the doors open and blocked her path. Her assailant jerked her backward against him, and his foul breath blasted her cheek.

"Almost missed it," the newcomer said in a German accent that bore an uncanny resemblance to Arnold Schwarzenegger's. "What floor do you want?"

Her captor tightened his grasp, as if warning her

to stay silent. His knife blade punctured her clothes and pierced her skin.

"Top floor," he said.

"Me, too." The German jabbed the panel with his gloved index finger.

Morgan crushed her snowballing panic and struggled to think. Was the German an accomplice? Or simply an unwitting tourist? She tried to catch his eye, but with his posture erect, he faced the doors, humming an annoyingly cheerful song under his breath. His imposing size would make him a valuable champion, but she had no idea how to gain his attention without provoking her captor to strike at the same time.

She had to think of something. If the German didn't help her, she was as good as dead.

The elevator bell dinged, and a black cloud of terror smothered her. They had reached the top floor of the parking garage, and she had missed her chance. The towering German was exiting. She steeled herself for the worst.

Suddenly the German twirled, grabbed her by the shoulders and tossed her out of the elevator against a nearby car.

Stunned, she slid to the ground. The German had saved her. Had he seen the knife at her back? She battled against the paralysis of fear. She had to get away.

Behind her, sounds of a struggle emanated from the elevator. A man roared in pain. Running feet pounded, a car door slammed, and tires screeched away on the concrete.

The acrid taste of terror blossomed in her mouth,

choking off her air. The man with the knife must have overpowered her German rescuer. But who had fled? The German, scared away, or her attacker?

Crawling on hands and knees between the cars, Morgan scurried to distance herself from her assailant. He'd been crazy with anger before. If he caught her now...

Panic pumped adrenaline through her, propelling her faster. Once she was far enough away, she would stand, run and search for a security guard. At the end of the parking row, she pushed to her feet.

And ran headlong into the German tourist.

Before she could react, he scooped her into his arms, flung her over his shoulder as easily as if she'd been a sack of feathers and headed across the garage and down the exit ramp at a sprint.

Shock turned her body to ice. She had eluded one attacker only to fall victim to another.

"Put me down!"

She beat his back with her fists. His steps never faltered, and her stomach bounced painfully against his rock-hard shoulder.

He loped down the ramp and, two floors below the roof, swerved into the garage past three rows of cars. Blood ran to her head, sickening her with dizziness and horror. Stopping before a battered blue Chevy, he tumbled her to her feet.

"Get in!" His accent had disappeared.

At all costs, she had to avoid entering the car, whose open door gaped like the jaws of death. Fighting back was her only hope. She landed a sharp kick to her captor's shin, heard with satisfaction his grunt of pained surprise and felt his grip ease.

She broke loose and ran.

But he was too fast for her. Strong hands grasped her shoulders and held her firm. She shrieked in outrage and fear, battling without effect.

Where were the security guards? Hadn't they heard her screams? Had Lashner sent the fake German as backup in case his knife-man failed? Or was the big man an independent maniac with his own motives?

Oh, Ben. Why didn't I listen to you?

When she opened her mouth to scream again, the German covered it with one large hand and with the other whipped her around to face him. Head down, she resisted his hold and wrestled to break loose.

"Look at me," he ordered.

She couldn't face him. Fear already threatened to steal her consciousness. If she looked into his eyes, she'd pass out. She had to keep fighting.

With massive strength, he pinned her against the car with his body, his leather-gloved hand still covering her mouth. Pressing her head back against the car, he forced her to confront him. She squeezed her eyes shut. As if struggling to escape on its own, her heart thrashed against her ribs, and a cold sweat drenched her body.

Would he kill her now and toss her off the parking garage as the other man had promised?

"Look at me!" His low voice reverberated in her head like a scream. "Now!"

I'm going to die.

A curious calmness, an acceptance of her fate, washed over her, and she lifted her eyes to his face.

Imprisoning her between the car and his powerful

body, one hand covering her mouth in an iron grip, he raised his free hand to his hair. With a quick tug, he discarded first a red wig, then the beard.

Her eyes widened with disbelief.

Chapter Three

"You!" Caught between anger and relief, Morgan steadied herself against the old car.

"No time to explain." Josh shoved her into the front passenger seat and raced around to the driver's seat. He plucked a baseball cap from the sun visor and crammed it on, pulling it low over his eyes. He thrust the red wig into her hands.

"Put this on," he ordered.

"But—"

"Don't argue." The fierceness in his voice sent tremors down her spine. "Lashner's man is still out there, looking for you. Blond hair makes you an easy target."

Josh's distinctive scent lingered on the wig, teasing her with memories of moonlight, a darkened room and her first encounter with the intriguing and infuriating man. "How did you know I was here?"

"Ben sent me."

Dear Ben.

First he'd saved her father's life, and now hers. She had been right to trust him. Too bad Ben wasn't well enough to rescue her himself and save her from the assault of emotions the mysterious Josh sent rocketing through her. She longed for Ben's calming influence as an antidote to Josh's electrifying presence.

While she forced the wig over her hair and tucked in trailing tendrils of telltale blond, Josh started the car and headed down the exit ramp.

"Stop!"

He slammed on the brakes. "What—"

"I'll miss my plane."

He shook his head in disbelief and launched the car down the ramp again.

"What about my luggage?"

"The airline can deliver it to Ben's tomorrow." His irritation sizzled in the enclosed space. "You still don't get it, do you?"

"If you think by forcing me to stay, I'm going to help you—"

"Morgan." His voice softened on her name. "Think about it. Lashner had someone watching the airport, waiting for you. He doesn't give a damn that you were returning to Memphis. He wants you *dead*."

The impact of his words left her struggling to inhale. "But if I can just get home to Memphis—"

"Lashner will have someone waiting there, as well. You know too much for him to let you live."

"Too much? About the fire? But I have no proof—"

"Not the fire." He eased the car into line at the parking garage tollbooth and slid lower in the seat, disguising his impressive height. "You and Ben are the only ones who know about the deficiencies of your father's discovery.''

''No, not the only ones.''

He turned and lifted his chin, riveting her with a compelling gaze beneath the bill of his cap. She hadn't noticed before the appealing coffee brown of his eyes.

''You told someone else?'' he asked.

''I told you.'' She caught his fleeting grimace of chagrin before he turned away.

His grip tightened on the steering wheel, straining the fine leather of his driving gloves. ''Too bad I couldn't hang on to the man who grabbed you. He might have given us the proof we need against Lashner.''

''He must have had a driver waiting, they pulled away so fast.'' She didn't want to think about her attacker. Her knees hadn't stopped shaking yet. If it hadn't been for Josh—

''Thank you. You saved my life.''

''All in a day's work, ma'am.''

She would have considered him too flippant over her narrow escape if she hadn't detected a hitch in his voice. Maybe he didn't have ice water in his veins, after all.

He reached the toll window, handed the attendant his ticket and money and, when the barricade lifted, steered into the airport exit lane.

Despite the subtlety of his movements, she detected his frequent checks in the rearview mirrors, and her heart hammered in her throat. ''Are we being followed?''

"Not that I can tell, but I didn't see the car Lashner's man escaped in. We'll have to stay alert."

His coolness steadied her, and she settled against the seat. "What difference does our knowing about the formula's deficiencies make? Any qualified chemist will soon discover its flaws."

"Not all chemists are as ethical as your father. For enough money, Lashner can bribe someone to falsify the findings. And without you or Ben to contradict the false report, nothing stands in the way of the board's approving the sale."

After the hit-and-run accident, her battered emotions had thrown her headlong into denial, and while she had accepted Ben's protection, she had refused to believe Lashner would hurt her. Now the reality of his intention to kill her, whether she remained in Florida or not, was finally sinking in, and with it, overwhelming apprehension.

"But isn't murdering us risky?" she asked. "Isn't he afraid of being caught?"

"He's already killed your father, so what does he have to lose? The State of Florida can only execute him once, no matter how many people he murders."

Josh's explanation chilled her. "We have to stop him. We should go to the police."

As if sensing her anxiety, he removed his right hand from the steering wheel and squeezed her shoulder with a reassuring pressure. "And tell them what?"

"I was attacked at the airport! You were a witness."

He withdrew his hand, and she felt abandoned at its absence.

"I can't connect your attacker to Lashner," he said. "Can you?"

Blinking away tears of frustration, she shook her head. "I never saw his face. But at least the police would be alerted to our suspicions."

"And so would Lashner." His square jaw, illuminated by a passing headlight, clamped so tightly a muscle in his cheek twitched.

Her head throbbed with fatigue and confusion. In her exhaustion, she yearned to slide across the seat and curl against Josh's warmth, but anxiety refused to let her rest. "How would going to the police tip off Lashner?"

"Gulfside is a small town with Chemco its major employer." He checked the rearview mirror again as he turned onto the interstate entry ramp. "Lashner has friends in high places, including the police department and city hall."

"Are you saying the Gulfside police are corrupt?" The possibility scared her into wakefulness.

"They're good men who regard Lashner as a pillar of the community." He pressed the accelerator and merged with the onslaught of traffic. "Without hard evidence, they'd consider any charge against Lashner a joke. Maybe even share a few laughs with Lashner himself about it."

"Surely Lashner knows we suspect him."

"Have you ever filed a complaint with a police department?" he asked.

"No."

"One of the first things they'll want to know is how and where to get in touch with you. Do you want Lashner tipped off that you're living at Ben's?"

"No." So she couldn't turn to the authorities. Silently she railed against her helplessness, until a glance at an approaching road sign accelerated her frustration into full-blown alarm. "We're headed *east?*"

"Right."

His amused look, under different circumstances, might have generated a responsive flutter in her heart. Her cardiac rhythm, however, had already attained warp speed when she realized they were barreling away from Gulfside. "Ben's house is the other way."

"We're taking the long way back." His mellow reasonableness slowed her racing pulse. "I want to be certain none of Lashner's hired guns are following us."

They left the outskirts of Tampa, traveling past dark pastures, deserted orange groves and empty strawberry fields, and her apprehension returned. She had only Josh's word that Ben had sent him. For all she knew... She thrust away notions too horrible to contemplate, and the effort made her tremble.

"You okay?"

"Sure," she answered, too brightly and too fast.

His scrutiny burned her cheeks, but, afraid to face him, she stared at the road. She wanted to trust him, to believe he would protect her as he had at the airport, but she had endured too much heartache and sustained too many shocks the past few days to suspend her skepticism now.

Her trembling increased until her teeth chattered.

"You're *not* okay." Josh pulled onto an off-ramp, followed the exit lane to a brightly lit restaurant and parked in the lot. He climbed out of the car, circled it and opened her door. "Come on. Something to eat and a cup of hot coffee will settle your nerves."

Dozens of cars in the lot and the crowd of people visible through the plate-glass windows quelled her shaking, but not her suspicions.

"I'm not hungry," she said, "but I need to use the rest room."

Without waiting for a response, she strode into the building, past the cashier's counter and into the alcove at the rear. Just as she had hoped, a pay phone hung on the wall outside the rest room doors. She had deposited a quarter and was dialing Ben's number when Josh caught up with her.

"What are you doing?" His sharp tone and surly expression projected the menace she remembered from their first meeting.

She tipped her head to face him. His eyes, shadowed by the cap, glowed almost black in the murky light.

"I'm calling Ben to let him know I'm okay."

An unreadable expression flitted across his face before he nodded. "Good idea. I'll meet you out front."

He sauntered away as the phone began to ring.

"Wells's residence," Harper's familiar voice answered.

"This is Morgan. Let me speak to Ben."

"I'm sorry, Mrs. Wells, but Mr. Wells has retired for the night."

The stiffness in his tone indicated he wouldn't wake his employer unless hell was freezing over. Maybe not even then.

"It's an emergency, Harper," she begged.

From the phone alcove, she observed Josh, pacing the parking lot in front of the restaurant impatiently. He could tramp a trench in the asphalt, but she would refuse to get back in the car unless Ben assured her she was safe.

"Did Mr. Josh find you?" Harper asked.

"Yes. How did you know?"

"Mr. Wells called him when you left this evening and asked him to follow you to the airport. Mr. Wells was afraid there might be trouble." Harper's statement was the longest she had heard the reserved man speak.

"Sending Josh after me was Ben's idea?"

"Yes, madam. He wanted Mr. Josh to bring you home." He cleared his throat as if uncertain what to say. "Mr. Wells meant home to Gulfside, not Memphis."

Relief shot through her like a geyser. Josh had told the truth. "Thanks, Harper. If Ben wakes up before I arrive, tell him Josh insists on taking the long way home."

She slumped against the wall with weariness and relief. Between the attack at the airport and the emotional trapeze she'd ridden back and forth from fearing Josh to trusting him, she had depleted her energy.

Josh was waiting.

With the last of her strength, she pushed away from the wall and stumbled into the rest room. At the lavatory, she splashed cold water on her face in an effort to stay awake. When she lifted her head, she almost screamed at the sight of the redheaded stranger who faced her.

She had forgotten she was wearing Josh's red wig.

Stifling a nervous giggle, she dried her face on a rough paper towel and tucked strands of blond hair under the band of the wig. Her nerves had quieted by the time she returned to the car.

She experienced a twinge of guilt at Josh's guileless smile as she slid onto the front seat and wondered if he had guessed her lack of trust.

"Ben was asleep," she said, "so I told Harper we'd be home soon."

"Sleep sounds like a good idea." The warmth in his brown eyes reminded her of melted caramels. He handed her his jacket from the back seat. "Use this as a pillow and try to rest."

Reassured by Harper's endorsement of Josh, Morgan folded the garment, tucked it next to the door and snuggled against it. Enveloped by the jacket's aroma of leather and Josh's soap, she drifted off to sleep.

MORGAN AWOKE when the car stopped before the soaring gates of Ben's waterfront estate.

"Sleep well?" Josh asked.

Yawning and stretching, she observed the delicate coral light playing on the high brick wall, the cool dawn breeze ruffling the leaves and the violet dome of sky above the gray slate roof of the house. She looked anywhere but at Josh to hide her pleasure at waking up to his heart-stopping smile.

"What time is it?"

"Almost six." Josh rolled down his window and punched a code into the security system panel beside the drive.

"It took *six* hours to drive thirty miles from Tampa?" Her sleepiness vanished.

He shrugged. "I wanted to be sure we weren't being tailed. I traveled south past Sarasota, then circled back over the Skyway Bridge."

An electronic hum sounded, followed by an audible click, and the gates swung wide in a slow arc. As Josh drove through, Morgan relaxed, safe again in Ben's haven on the bluff above the Gulf of Mexico. Formidable ten-foot brick walls, softened with tropical greenery, surrounded the grounds. The wrought-iron gates provided the only access to the multiacre estate. Lashner would need a small army to breach Ben's barricades.

She climbed out of Josh's ancient car on wobbly legs and surveyed the house, a Norman château set incongruously on Florida's gulf coast. Bougainvillea twined around twin turrets that flanked the main house, and the prolific vines, heavy with magenta blossoms, covered the front walls and clambered onto the high-pitched roof.

Taking three steps to Josh's one, she approached the double oak doors of the front entrance. Josh raised his hand, but the doors opened before he could knock.

Harper, his impressive six-foot-six bulk immaculately attired in a dark blue suit and tie, greeted her with a neutral expression that looked carved from honey-colored wood. "Welcome home, Mrs. Wells. Good morning, sir."

Accompanied by Josh, she stepped past Harper into the entry. Her vision adjusted slowly to the dimness of the dark-paneled entrance hall with its wide,

soaring staircase, and her footsteps echoed against
the terra-cotta tiles.

Harper preceded them and flung open double
doors opposite the entrance. Daylight flooded the
foyer, blinding her as it had a week ago when she
first met Ben Wells. With Josh at her elbow, she
entered the airy living room with its western expanse
of glass walls offering a panoramic view of the terrace and gardens, distant sand dunes fringed with sea
oats, and finally the shining waters of the gulf. Several glass panels had been rolled into their wall re-
cesses, and draperies of English chintz billowed in
the sea air.

"Mrs. Denny," Harper said, "is preparing your
breakfast."

Morgan nodded. Everything, the overstuffed fur-
niture in rose-patterned chintz, the vases of fresh
flowers, the subdued colors of the Aubusson carpets,
appeared normal. But something was—different. Her
nerves tingled with alarm.

Something was *wrong*.

"Is Ben awake?" she asked.

"No, madam, Mr. Wells is sleeping in this morning."

She would have accepted his statement if she
hadn't detected the peculiar glance that passed between Josh and Harper. Anxiety ballooned in her
chest.

Before either man could stop her, she rushed to
the far end of the room and flung open the door to
the guest wing, which Ben had appropriated for easy
wheelchair access after the accident. In the massive
bedroom, sunlight streamed past open draperies, il-

luminating the brocade coverlet of the empty bed, and the motorized wheelchair, also empty. The door to the adjoining bath stood open. It, too, was empty.

Tears stung her eyes. She spun back toward the door, where Josh and Harper blocked the way.

"He isn't—" She couldn't say the word. "His injuries didn't—"

"Mr. Wells," Harper said, "is alive and well."

Relief rushed through her, but suspicion came hard on its heels. "Then, where is he?"

Harper observed her with his usual immobile expression, but Josh's face reflected guilt, discomfort and another emotion she couldn't name.

The aura of safety that had surrounded her since entering the gates evaporated like mist beneath a hot sun. Ben, her protector, was gone, and the pair who might have conspired against him stood between her and her only route of escape.

Almost crippled by terror, she refused to give them the satisfaction of knowing they'd frightened her. She balled her hands on her hips, lifted her chin in defiance and stared straight into Josh's deceitful brown eyes.

"Where's Ben?" Anger blistered her voice. "What have you done with my husband?"

"What have *I* done?" Josh rolled his gaze skyward, spread his hands and shook his head. "Why are you asking me? I've been with you all night, remember?"

He turned to Ben's bulky manservant. "Where is he, Harper?"

The valet's inscrutable countenance melted into an expression of bewilderment. "Mr. Wells—"

"Never mind," Josh said. "You're a man of few words under the best of circumstances, and you've already been up all night. Go on to bed, and I'll fetch Mrs. Denny to explain."

Before Morgan could object, Josh was striding toward the kitchen wing.

Harper's emotionless mask was back in place. "If there's nothing else, Mrs. Wells—"

"No, thank you, Harper." She dismissed him with a tired wave.

He executed a dignified semibow and withdrew.

Certain something was out of sync but unable to put her finger on it, Morgan wandered back into the living room. She longed for rest but was too agitated from unanswered questions to remain in one place. She crossed the threshold of the sliding glass doors and paced the flagstone terrace.

Dazzling sunlight exploded like laser bursts on the gulf's gentle swells, and the calm perfection of the early morning made last night's terror seem only a bad dream. Leaning on the stone balustrade that surrounded the terrace, she inhaled the salt air and attempted to analyze her fears.

The tranquil setting did little to calm her jitters. She flinched as if she'd been slapped when a hand grasped her elbow.

"Come and sit," Josh said.

She followed him to a table in a shaded corner. The heavy fragrance of honeysuckle vines from a nearby arbor filled the air, and her rebellious stomach lurched at their cloying sweetness.

"Mrs. Denny is bringing breakfast," Josh said. "She'll explain about Ben."

Breakfast was the last thing Morgan wanted. Skittish with forced wakefulness and the curious excitement Josh's presence aroused in her, she perched on the edge of a patio chair.

Josh slipped onto a seat across from her, and while she avoided his eyes, she could feel his gaze assessing her.

"Are you all right?" he asked.

"I'm fine." Unable to target the source of her skittishness, she couldn't have explained it, even if she'd wanted to.

Mrs. Denny appeared with a silver coffee service. Behind her, a middle-aged maid carried a breakfast tray. The housekeeper poured their coffee in silence while the maid arranged plates and silverware, bowls of sliced melon and a basket of miniature blueberry crumb cakes on the linen-draped table.

After the maid left, Mrs. Denny spoke. "You are not to worry about Mr. Wells, ma'am. He has checked into the hospital for more tests—"

"But he didn't tell me," Morgan protested.

The housekeeper's mouth flexed into a thin line of disapproval, and her gray eyes glittered like dirty ice. "Begging your pardon, ma'am, but you did not give him time to tell you anything before you left last night."

"Which hospital is he in?" Josh asked.

"Only Harper knows," Mrs. Denny replied. "Mr. Wells checked in under a false name in the middle of the night, so no one, except his doctor, knows who he really is. He says he is safer that way."

Morgan felt a stirring of fear for her protector.

"Are you sure he's there only for tests? He isn't worse?"

"Mr. Wells has suffered no setback," Mrs. Denny assured her in a softer tone.

With an odd expression, Josh continued to scrutinize Morgan. "Don't tell me you've grown fond of your new husband."

"Of course I'm fond of him. I—" Heat rose to her face, and she changed the subject. "Can I phone him, Mrs. Denny? Did he leave a number?"

The older woman shook her head. "He said if Mr. Josh was successful in bringing you home, he would call you later today. Now, if you have everything you need…"

"Yes, thank you," Morgan said.

The housekeeper, her back ramrod straight, pivoted and marched back into the house.

Josh drank coffee and eyed Morgan over the top of his cup. "Satisfied now?"

"About Ben?"

He nodded. A sliver of sunshine pierced the shade and illuminated the web of lines at the corners of his eyes. A fine white edge bordered the taut set of his mouth, and the usual bronze cast of his tan had paled. He was as worn-out as she was.

Embarrassment stung her. He had risked his life to save her, been up all night, and she had thanked him by accusing him of kidnapping Ben.

But she couldn't conquer her distrust. Something about Josh continually stirred her suspicions as well as her senses. As weary as he appeared, he remained cautious and aloof, as if he guarded secrets no one else could share. He had refused to divulge his last name. What else was he hiding?

"Why do you do this?" she asked.

"This?"

"Work for Ben."

He inclined his head toward her plate. "You're not eating."

Automatically she selected a cake from the basket and placed it on her plate. "Is it the money?"

"I wouldn't relish this particular assignment for any amount of money," he said with a grimace of distaste, "although Ben always pays well."

She forced a smile and tried not to take his rejection personally. "Is it the danger you find attractive?"

"No, not the danger."

His eyes, a honey brown flecked with the gold of reflected sunlight, probed hers, and she experienced the ridiculous whimsy that she could tumble into their depths and fall forever without hitting bottom.

Fidgeting beneath his concentrated gaze, she grasped her fork and picked at her crumb cake. "It's none of my business—"

"Since my job involves protecting you, you have every right to ask." His voice was warm. Turning away, he stared across the gardens toward the gulf and displayed the stunning profile that had impressed her the night they met.

His words indicated a willingness to respond to her queries, but his detached demeanor emitted the reticence she had come to expect. She was too tired to attempt to drag answers from him now.

Exhaustion, grief, concern for Ben, memories of

last night's terror at the airport and a primal attraction to the enigmatic man across the table converged in a wave of vertigo. She clasped the fine china cup with both hands and gulped hot black coffee, which hit her roiling stomach like molten lava.

Josh rose to his feet with a sluggishness that proclaimed his weariness. Leaning across the table, he traced the curve of her cheek with his finger. "Get some sleep. When we meet tonight, I'll answer your questions."

He turned to leave, and his leather jacket fell open. Below his right collarbone, a dark, spreading stain soaked the front of his chambray shirt.

He was bleeding.

Fatigue forgotten, she jumped from her chair and rushed to him. "You're hurt!"

"What?"

"There—" she shoved aside his jacket "—you're bleeding."

He glanced at the bloodstain without surprise. "Lashner's creep must have nicked me with his knife when we struggled in the parking garage."

He flashed her a self-deprecating smile, as if being knifed was an unremarkable occurrence, and once more turned to go.

"Shouldn't you take care of that?" She grabbed his arm. "I could clean and bandage—"

"I'll see to it." He spoke with unfamiliar sharpness, wrenched from her grasp and strode away across the terrace.

When he reached the living room, he didn't turn to say goodbye.

WHEN MORGAN AWAKENED later that day, she threw back the coverlet and slipped from the queen-size bed. Her luggage, delivered by the airline, sat on a blanket chest at the foot of the four-poster.

She drew open pale rose draperies and stepped through French doors onto a broad balcony that faced the gulf. The sun neared the horizon and colored clouds and surf with amazing tropical hues of tangerine, mango and papaya.

Sunset.

She had slept more than ten hours.

A freshening wind whipped her thin cotton gown and drove away the last dregs of sleep. Her body felt rested, but her spirit struggled with the same burden of questions and emotions she had carried to bed.

Abandoning the balcony, she surveyed the enormous bedroom that had been hers since her arrival more than a week ago. She could fit her entire Memphis apartment between its walls. Her little place in Tennessee seemed a million miles and a hundred years away.

Had it really been less than two weeks since her father's funeral? She fought back tears, remembering the man who had been both mother and father after her mom had died of breast cancer when Morgan was fifteen.

Sinking onto the edge of the bed, she buried her face in her hands. In the past ten years, she had spent only summer and Christmas holidays with her father, believing they had a lifetime ahead to enjoy more time with each other.

Now Robert Lashner had murdered him and stolen all their days together. Frank Winters would never walk his daughter down the aisle, hold his first grand-child, enjoy the well-earned retirement he had saved for all his life.

Anger crowded out her grief and overran fear. Since the attack at the airport, she had abandoned the idea that she could simply walk away from Lashner. Motivations jammed her mind, bunching and over-lapping. She attempted to arrange them by priority, but they were so intertwined, sorting seemed futile. If anyone were to ask why she wanted to fight Lash-ner and prove his guilt, her answer had to be three-fold: to avenge her father, to stay alive and to make certain Lashner, either through his assassins or his misuse of her father's discovery, didn't murder any-one else.

Working with Josh made her uneasy, but if helping him was the only way to bring Robert Lashner to justice, she would do whatever he asked.

Tonight she would meet with Josh again. This time she would agree to his plan.

Chapter Four

"I haven't picked so much shrapnel out of one man since Vietnam," Dr. Tom Hendrix, Ben's longtime friend and physician, stood by the hospital room window, shaking his head at his patient.

"I feel like I've been to war," Ben admitted.

"You were lucky to survive that explosion, but that doesn't mean you're out of the woods. Bust that wound open again and you could bleed to death."

Ben smiled at his friend's ferocity but said nothing. After Tom's intensive tests and treatments, talking hurt.

"Go home to bed," Tom said, "and *stay* in bed until that wound is completely healed."

"Can't do that. I have too much to do."

The doctor with the build of a marine and the bedside manner of a porcupine uttered a disparaging noise, somewhere between a growl and a snort. "Then you can add burial plans to your to-do list, because if you don't take better care of yourself, you'll be the star attraction at a funeral."

Ben swung his legs to the side of the bed, taking care not to flinch at the pain, shrugged into his shirt and began fastening buttons. "I'm counting on you to keep me going."

"In the immortal words of Bones McCoy, I'm a doctor, not a magician." Tom raked his fingers through his shaggy gray mane. "Why are you so intent on making that new wife of yours a widow?"

Ben failed to suppress a wince as the shirt rubbed his bandages. "Frank Winters was your friend, too, Tom."

Memories of Frank deluged Ben. Long, lazy evenings of chess, congenial conversation, imported beer. Grueling, sweaty racquetball duels. Frank's astute counsel over problems at Chemco, and his warm, gut-deep laugh, often at himself as the butt of his own jokes.

Frank had treated him like a son, had even tried to include him in family celebrations when Morgan came to visit, but Ben had always declined, reluctant to intrude. If he'd known how Morgan would affect him, he would have accepted Frank's invitations years ago.

Now Frank was gone.

Forever.

"I've told you Frank's death was no accident," Ben said. "If I can't prove Robert Lashner's behind it, Morgan and I both will die, no matter how much care I take."

Tom perched on the broad windowsill and crossed his arms over his white coat. "You're still convinced the police can't handle this?"

"Lashner leaves his dirty work to hired thugs, and I want Lashner to be the one to pay. When I have evidence that ties him directly to Frank's death, then I'll go to the police."

"And in the meantime?"

"I'm not in this alone. And I'll rest as much as I can."

Tom's mournful expression brightened. "I met Frank's daughter at the funeral. She's a knockout."

"I won't argue with that." Ben gingerly tugged on a pair of chinos and tucked in his shirt.

"I guess I should be thankful your marriage is a sham." Tom's vivid eyes flashed above his leering grin, and he wiggled his thick brows. "If you were a bona fide newlywed, you'd be overexerting yourself day and night and wouldn't live out the week."

Ben laughed, and the action skewered him with fresh agony. "You're not a doctor, Tom, you're a dirty old man. Now, get out of here so I can call Morgan and tell her my tests came out fine."

The door closed behind the doctor and Ben reached for the phone. He'd never been able to hide anything from the shrewd and knowing eyes of Tom Hendrix, but this time he'd managed. Even his old friend hadn't guessed the depth of his feelings for Morgan Winters or that he would move heaven and earth to keep her safe, no matter how much pain and personal risk he suffered.

Even if saving her was the last thing he ever did.

A BIZARRE FEELING of déjà vu descended on Morgan as she rode down the lighted streets of Gulfside beside the red-haired, red-bearded Josh in his battered old Chevy. With her hair tucked beneath a billed cap pulled low over her face, she watched Josh check the rearview mirror to see if they'd been followed from their rendezvous point in the crowded grocery store parking lot.

Except for Josh's disguise and their surreptitious meeting, the outing reminded her of dates she'd had in high school. The same tingling anticipation those occasions had triggered, only a hundred times stronger, consumed her. Josh and the accompanying danger proved a heady combination.

"Ben called before dinner," she said. "The doctor says he's recovering as he should be and can come home tomorrow."

Josh kept his eyes on the road. "Maybe by then we'll have some progress to report. Did you bring the keys?"

"Right here." Morgan patted the pocket of her jeans. "What are you looking for at Dad's condo?"

"Notes to prove the instability of his last discovery or anything that could incriminate Lashner."

The prospect of searching through her father's belongings saddened her. "Wouldn't Dad have kept everything about the formula in his office at the plant?"

"I'm sure Lashner cleaned out anything incriminating from your father's office immediately after the explosion."

"Wouldn't he have searched the condo, too?"

"Maybe. But the condo is in a gated community with the best security service available. Breaking in would be tough." He turned to her with a glint of humor in his eyes. "We'll be lucky if they let us in."

Even framed by the ridiculous red beard, his smile caused a happy flip-flop in her stomach. Or else her body was reminding her she had eaten little breakfast and had only picked at dinner.

"Do you suppose Lashner has someone watching Dad's place in case I show up?"

He jerked her cap over her nose with a playful tug. "That, my dear Watson, is why I'm in disguise and your face and hair are hidden."

At a traffic signal, he slowed to a stop. In the muted glare of the streetlights, he appeared rested but restless. A trace of reserve suggested he was holding something back, and his secretiveness gave rise to her persistent uneasiness.

When the signal changed, Josh pressed the gas. The car sped away from the lighted intersection, and the interior plunged into pitch-blackness, alleviated only by the glow from the dash lights. The weak illumination cast disfiguring shadows on his handsome face, reminding her of scary games she had played as a child, using darkness and a flashlight angled beneath her chin to create a monster and frighten her playmates.

A shiver whisked through her.

Josh was no monster, so why was she suspicious of him? He *had* saved her life.

Ben trusts him, she reminded herself, *and so should I.*

Watching the black ribbon of road uncurl before the headlights, she slumped in her seat and examined her conflicting reactions to the man at her side. Maybe the overpowering pull she experienced whenever they were together triggered her uncertainties.

Years ago, beginning after her mother's death, she had become adept at maintaining emotional distance between herself and others. So adept that she had prevented her father from becoming too close as well, especially when she had stayed in Memphis after he took his job with Chemco.

But with Josh, she had been unsuccessful at erecting barriers. His attractiveness, combined with the current danger, made her rebellious heart beat faster and her breathing quicken whenever he appeared. His enigmatic behavior enticed her to solve the riddle of what lay beneath that roguishly handsome exterior.

She never had been able to resist a puzzle.

She smiled, remembering the handsome film star she once idolized until a Barbara Walters interview revealed him as silly and shallow, proving familiarity often bred contempt.

Perhaps if she could peel back Josh's mysterious facade, he, too, would be less compelling. Not shallow or silly, she was certain, but at least only an ordinary man.

A *resistible* man.

She sat up, turned toward him and leaned against the passenger door for a better view of his reactions. "You promised this morning you would answer all my questions tonight."

"Did I say *all?* I must have been punch-drunk from lack of sleep. A man has to have *some* secrets."

"But you don't have to compete with the CIA." Her sarcasm popped out automatically, and she wished she had put her mind in gear before opening her mouth.

He glanced at her quickly, then returned his attention to the road. "Is that how you see me?"

She attempted a laugh, which emerged thin and

feeble. "You haven't been a fountain of information. When I'm with you, I seem to do all the talking."

He stared straight ahead, but the corner of his mouth elevated. "You're blaming me because you're a chatterbox?"

"You know what I mean." His friendly crack pleased her, and she socked him playfully on the shoulder.

He gasped at the impact, and his face twisted in pain.

"Sorry." The intensity of his reflex alarmed her. Her abductor at the airport must have wounded him worse than she'd realized. "I guess I don't know my own strength."

"I pulled a muscle lugging you through the parking garage last night." An oncoming car illuminated a twinkle in his eyes, and his grimace gradually relaxed. "Actually, considering the substantial burden, I probably pulled quite a few muscles."

"Flattery will get you nowhere."

She felt more comfortable with him at this instant than she had since they met. Had he guessed her apprehensions and tried to quiet her worries with his teasing? Or was he allowing her a peek at the real Josh for the first time?

She leaned back and closed her eyes. Even when he wasn't being secretive, he presented her with new mysteries.

"I thought you had questions for me," he said.

She opened her eyes and straightened in her seat. "If, as you said this morning, it isn't for the money or the danger, why are you working for Ben?"

His handsome profile settled into hard lines, like

the granite face of a cliff sheared by blasting. "Frank Winters was my friend. Ben's my friend. I owe it to both of them to see that Frank's killer is brought to justice."

That answer, at least, seemed straightforward enough.

"Have you known Ben long?" she asked.

"All my life."

"What's he like?"

Josh raised his eyebrows. "What's wrong with this picture? You're the one who's married to the guy."

She resisted the urge to sock him again. "I'm serious. Ben tires so easily, I haven't had a chance to really talk with him. What's the harm in your filling me in?"

Josh slowed at the intersection, turned west and headed across the causeway to Gulfside Beach where her father's condo was located. "What do you want to know?"

"Anything. Everything. I know Ben was much younger than my father, but they enjoyed each other's company. They played chess once a week, and racquetball."

Josh nodded. "Not only was Frank Ben's friend, he was like a father to him. Ben never really knew his own father. His parents were killed in a boating accident when he was eight. He was raised by an elderly uncle who died while Ben was away at college."

Ben had told Morgan he'd always lived in the Norman-style mansion. She pictured him as a small boy wandering through the long hallways and cavernous rooms of his impressive house. "He must have been lonely."

"He still is," Josh said quietly.

"Why didn't he marry?"

Josh was silent for such a long time, she had decided he wasn't going to answer when he finally spoke. "Ben has a hard time trusting people."

"That doesn't track with my impression of him."

Josh shrugged. "He felt abandoned by his parents when they died. When his uncle passed away, he discovered the old man had misappropriated most of the revenues from Ben's trust."

"Ouch. That must have hurt."

"Ben didn't have time for bitterness. He had to work hard and smart to keep from losing his family home. When he founded Chemco Industries with Robert Lashner, he believed he'd finally gained financial security and a partner he could depend on."

Sympathy for her husband poured through her. "So Lashner's betrayal was the unkindest cut of all."

"That's one way of putting it." Josh's expression was grim. "Even before your father's murder, Ben suspected Lashner of mishandling Chemco's funds."

"It's no wonder Ben doesn't trust anyone," she said, "but he trusts you."

Josh shot her an engaging grin. "I've never given him a reason not to."

Morgan turned and stared north across Gulfside Bay's dark waters where the lights of Ben's house flickered like distant stars on the high bluff. She had believed Ben Wells trusted her. He had taken her into his home. Good grief, he had even *married* her. That his actions weren't based on trust had never occurred to her. Now she realized he could have wanted her close to keep an eye on her. Maybe he had her working with Josh for the same reason. Was Josh a guardian—or a spy?

"What about me?" she asked.

"I've never given you a reason not to trust me, either, have I?"

Josh had either misunderstood her question or intentionally sidestepped it. She closed her eyes and remembered her father. Evidently, he had trusted both Ben and Josh. If she intended to see his murderer brought to justice, she had no choice but to trust them, too, whether they reciprocated that trust or not.

She didn't answer Josh's question.

JOSH BROUGHT THE CHEVY to a stop at the gate of the condominium complex and remained in the car's shadows. The security guard, a tall bulky man with the build of an aging football player, stepped close to the window.

"Give me the apartment number," the uniformed guard said, "and I'll call for clearance."

Morgan leaned toward the driver's window and pushed her cap off her face. "It's Morgan Winters, Burt. We're going to Dad's apartment, number 253."

"Sure, I remember you, Miss Winters. I'm awful sorry about your dad. He was a great guy."

"Thanks, Burt."

With her face so close, Josh savored the exotic fragrance of her perfume and watched tears well in her eyes at the guard's condolences. He quashed the longing to console her. The sooner they were out of the bright, public glare of the entrance lights, the better. Lashner was certain to have a man staking out Frank's residence in hopes Morgan would appear.

Burt stepped back and lifted the striped bar that blocked the drive. Josh sped through and circled the building to Frank's parking place on the opposite side.

"You've been here before," Morgan said with a hint of surprise.

"I picked up your Dad when we played racquetball. And sometimes Frank would have me over for grouper he'd broil on the grill on his balcony."

"But Burt didn't recognize you." Her voice oozed suspicion.

"I'm in disguise, remember?" He parked in a space marked "visitor" and killed the engine. "And I kept my face averted. Burt would have wondered what the heck was going on if he'd realized the red-haired guy was me."

Josh yanked off the wig and beard and combed his fingers through his hair. The movement caused his chest to ache worse than a tooth with an exposed nerve.

Damn Lashner and his hired thugs. They were wearing him down.

The night had barely begun, and too many nights without sleep were catching up with him. He was already tired. Tired of being wary, of screening every word in case he revealed too much, of sneaking around in an itchy disguise, of lying—

"Are you coming?"

Morgan's question jerked him from his silent grumblings. She had exited the car and circled to the driver's door. When she removed her cap and shook out her hair, pale light from the tropical moon turned her golden tresses silver and illuminated her face with a magical sheen.

He had forgotten how petite she was, only slightly taller than the roof of the car. As she stood waiting, awash in moonbeams, with her hands propped on slender hips and head cocked to one side, she looked diminutive and fragile, as ethereal as a dream.

Given the chance, Robert Lashner would squash her like a bug.

The disturbing image drove away his fatigue and propelled him from the car. "Want to take the stairs or the elevator?"

"The stairs are closer." She pivoted on her heel and trudged toward the end of the building, her sneakers crunching on the graveled path.

Despite his fatigue, he issued a silent prayer of thanks, not knowing if he could have trusted himself not to touch her in the intimate confines of the small elevator, even for a ride up only one floor.

"Hey, Watson," he called, "wait for me."

She turned, and his breath lodged in his throat at her smile, incandescent in the moonlight. Blaming his light-headedness on lack of sleep, he plodded past her onto the open stairs.

At the second-floor landing, he stepped to the railing of the open hallway. From that elevation, he could view the parking lot and the street beyond the privacy walls. With a sweeping glance, he checked parked cars for signs of anyone watching and searched the puddles of shade along the sidewalks for a lurking figure.

Nothing moved inside the cars or in the shadows of the trees.

But just because he couldn't spot someone, didn't mean a lookout wasn't there.

Josh turned quickly and covered the few feet between him and Frank's front door, where Morgan wrestled with the key. As he reached her, the stiff lock yielded and she stepped inside. He followed and locked the door behind him.

Morgan flicked the light switch in the entry hall that turned on matching table lamps in the living room. "Someone's been here."

Expecting to find the condo tossed and trashed, he scanned the room, but everything stood neatly in place. Exactly as he remembered. "Looks fine to me."

Shaking her head, she stepped through the door on her right into the kitchen and turned on the light. "No, someone's been taking care of the place. It doesn't have the musty smell of a house that's been closed for almost three weeks."

She crossed to the pass-through window that opened onto the dining area and reached into the ceramic pot of a large, healthy fern. "Someone's watered the plants."

She wheeled and yanked open the refrigerator door. "And the refrigerator's been cleaned out. No moldy food or spoiled milk."

Josh wrinkled his forehead. "Maybe Frank's attorney—"

"He gave me his only key."

With lightning speed, Josh slapped the light switch and swamped the kitchen with darkness. In the same movement, he dragged Morgan close and drew his gun from the holster at his back.

"Don't make another sound," he whispered against her ear.

A rush of adrenaline washed away his fatigue, and his blood rumbled in his ears. No wonder he'd spotted no one on the street. Somehow Lashner had obtained a key and placed someone inside to wait for Morgan's arrival. With her clasped against him, he sidled back to the entrance hall and placed his lips against her hair.

"Wait here. If you hear me yell—" he released her long enough to press his car keys into her hand "—run like hell to the car and drive straight to Ben's."

"But—"

"No arguments." He tightened his grip on her shoulders. "Just do as I say."

She nodded, and the soft silkiness of her hair brushed his face like a kiss.

He released her and advanced several feet down the hallway, groped to his left around the door frame and flipped on the lights of the spare bedroom that had doubled as Frank's study. With his gun at the ready, he swung into the room.

Empty.

He crossed quickly to the louvered bi-fold doors of the closet and flung them back.

Only stacked boxes, winter clothes on hangers and an assortment of odds and ends filled the closet.

A quick check of the adjoining bathroom also revealed no one. Josh crossed hurriedly through the obviously deserted living room, searched Frank's bedroom and bath, then the balcony that overlooked the water.

Satisfied no one lurked in the apartment, he called to Morgan. "All clear. Whoever was here is gone."

He secured the sliding glass doors and turned to find Morgan in the middle of the living room, hands rammed in the back pockets of her jeans, straining her small, firm breasts against the silk fabric of her azure blouse.

"This is the first time I've been here since Dad's...accident," she said with a tremor in her voice. "I couldn't...it seems strange, empty, without him."

Josh slid his automatic into its holster, not knowing what to say to relieve her pain. Her love for her father was obvious, and its depth equaled that of her loss.

She gazed at him through unshed tears. "When Dad took the job at Chemco, he wanted to buy a big, roomy house and have me live with him."

"Why didn't you?"

"I was eighteen and reveling in my first taste of independence. I wanted to stay in Memphis with my friends. After all, I assumed I had the rest of my life to enjoy my father's company."

"If it's any comfort, I think he understood."

She paused in her inspection of the room. "Dad talked to you about me?"

"All the time. He was very proud of his little girl." Josh nodded toward a picture on the television of a young Morgan in shorts and T-shirt, her face freckled, knees skinned, her wide smile exposing a mouthful of metal.

"Dad bought his condo furnished. I never figured him as a tropical-prints-and-rattan kind of guy, but he managed to put his own stamp on the place." She picked up a mahogany piece from the chess set on the coffee table and ran her fingers over the intricately carved queen.

For several minutes, he watched her wander through the apartment, handling her father's belongings, confronting her loss. With all that had happened since Frank's death, Morgan had had little time to mourn. He regretted he couldn't grant more now.

"We have to hurry," he said. "Whoever was here could return any moment."

"Sorry." She replaced Frank's pipe, his one vice, in its stand on the table beside his recliner and cleared her throat. "Where should we start?"

Her brave expression barely covered her pain, and the desire to hold her drove a white-hot spike of longing through his gut. But even if they'd had the time, he doubted she would appreciate his solace.

She still didn't trust him. And with good reason.

"Did your father keep a journal?"

She looked embarrassed. "I don't know."

"A journal or diary might be helpful. Look for one, and for anything relating to Chemco." He swore silently at the sentiment in his voice. Morgan's grief and his own return to Frank's familiar rooms had affected him more than he'd bargained for.

"Anything else?" she asked.

"I noticed an empty box in the study closet. We can load what we find in it. I'll take the study, you search the bedroom."

After almost an hour of flipping through books and

the neatly arranged files in the built-in desk unit of Frank's study, Josh admitted defeat. Not a scrap of paper contained a single reference to the gasoline substitute or Robert Lashner. Frank must have kept all relevant data at his office, where Lashner would have stolen it after the fire.

His sagging spirits lifted when Morgan entered the study with her arms filled with books, letters and papers. He swiveled the desk chair toward her. "You found something!"

"Yes." Her face radiated a bittersweet elation. "Wonderful things."

She dumped her burden on the bed and began sorting. "Photograph albums, letters Dad and Mom wrote to each other while he was in Vietnam—"

Disappointment filled him. Morgan had found family treasures, but obviously nothing that would help nail Frank's killer.

"And Dad's journals."

"Journals?" His expectations re-ignited.

Her unforgettable eyes sparkled with excitement. "From the time my father was eighteen, he kept a daily record. I brought only the years since he moved to Florida."

He shifted from the chair to the bed and patted the spread beside him. "Let me see this year's."

"That's the odd part." She settled next to him. "This year's journal isn't with the rest. Do you suppose he kept it at the office?"

His newfound hope sputtered and died. "If he did, Lashner has destroyed it by now."

She gazed up at him, still cradling her father's journals against her heart. Her mournful expression softened her delicate mouth and deepened the startling blue of her eyes. "So we've come up empty-handed."

"I wouldn't say that." He ignored the tender emotions swelling in his chest and pointed to the books and papers scattered across the bed. "Let's pack these to take back to Ben's. From the look on your face when you carried them in, I'm sure you'll agree they made the trip worthwhile."

He stood, raised his arms over his head to ease muscles knotted from leaning over Frank's desk, then bent once more to pack Morgan's treasures.

"Sh!" She grabbed his arm. "What was that?"

Instantly alert, he laid the letters and albums he held on the bed and reached for his gun.

A scrabbling sounded outside Frank's door, keys jingled and someone muttered in a low voice.

Lashner's man had returned.

Josh threw his arm around Morgan and tugged her toward the open doors of the closet. Once they had squeezed inside, he folded the doors shut, clutched her against him with one arm and, with the other, aimed his automatic toward the bedroom door.

The front doorknob rattled violently.

He'd been a fool to bring Morgan with him, but he had figured gaining entrance to Frank's place would be easier with her along. Now, instead of finding something to incriminate Lashner, he'd only succeeded in placing Morgan in danger.

The rattling at the front door increased, and he held his breath. Someone was fiddling with the stiff lock. He drew Morgan tighter. The sudden sensation of her pounding heart against his arm unnerved him like an electric shock. If ever he didn't need the distraction of her exhilarating nearness, it was now.

Attempting to ignore the feathery contact of her hair against his skin and the suppleness of her hips fused against him, he pressed his face against the space between the louvers until he could see the open bedroom door.

He cursed his luck. A confrontation with Lashner's thug would be totally nonproductive. Even if he captured the man and took him to the police, they'd have no reason to charge him, other than for trespassing.

Josh remembered his disguise, lying on the front seat of the car. He would have tipped his hand and revealed his identity for nothing.

But capturing Lashner's man was the best scenario the night had to offer.

He didn't want to think about the worst.

The front door opened and banged against the entry wall.

Josh flipped the safety off his gun and waited.

Chapter Five

Morgan cringed and jammed her fist against her mouth to keep from crying out when the front door struck the wall. Memories of the voice of her vicious abductor at the airport echoed in her mind, sending perspiration trickling down her backbone. Without the protective support of Josh's strong arm, she would have crumpled to the floor from the buckling of her knees.

Josh, however, seemed to take the intruder's entry in stride. He hadn't flinched at the noise. She would have known. Her body molded every one of his muscles in an embrace so intimate, if she hadn't been terrified, she might have embarrassed herself by doing something really stupid. Like standing on tiptoe to kiss the handsome scowl off his lips and run her fingers through his thick, dark hair.

But fear had an amazing way of clearing her mind, even of a temptation as provocative as Josh. Pressing her eye against an opening in the louvers, she braced herself for a glimpse of the new arrival.

Muttering softly, the newcomer closed the door,

approached the bedroom with an erratic, shuffling gait and stepped across the threshold.

Morgan's breath whistled through her teeth in surprise. Hovering in the doorway was a tiny woman, stooped and frail, who had to be eighty if she was a day. Her bright eyes, magnified to owllike proportions by thick glasses, swept the room, taking in the books and letters strewn across the bed and the desk drawers standing ajar.

"Oh, dear. Oh, my..."

Dismay sounded in the old woman's breathless voice, and she clasped a wrinkled hand, spotted with age, against her heart. Morgan didn't know her but was certain she hadn't been hired by Lashner. The woman turned and disappeared into the hallway in the direction of the living room.

Morgan felt the tension drain from Josh's muscles, but he didn't loosen his embrace. Without the distraction of imminent death, her blood began to simmer again, making immediate escape mandatory.

She stood on tiptoe and whispered in his ear. "I'll speak to her."

He turned to face her. For a searing instant his eyes burned into hers and his lips lingered so close to her mouth she could taste their heat. Too soon he released her and holstered his gun.

Breathless from that brief encounter, she slipped from the closet. Josh closed the door behind her.

"Hello," she called out in what she hoped sounded like a cheerful greeting. "Is somebody here?"

She rushed into the living room just as the old woman was exiting the master bedroom.

"Who—" The woman's weathered face creased into a warm smile. "You're Morgan. I should have guessed it was you."

"Yes. Have we met?"

The woman bobbed her head, bouncing soft waves of white hair. "At the funeral. But you might not remember, there were so many people. I'm Esther Clark. From next door."

"Would you like to sit down? I'm afraid I must have startled you."

"No, I won't stay. I looked after the place whenever your father was away, and when he died, I couldn't bear to see his plants wither and the dust collect." She handed Morgan a key on a chain with a plastic disk advertising a local pizza parlor. "But now you're here."

"Thanks for taking care of the place," Morgan said. "You've been very kind."

"No, love." She patted Morgan's hand. "It was your father who was kind. Any spot of trouble, from a burned-out bulb to a tripped circuit breaker, and he fixed it for me, straight away. Checking on his apartment seemed little enough in return for all his favors."

"I'm sure he considered you a very good neighbor, Mrs. Clark." Morgan walked toward the front door in hopes the woman would follow.

Esther tottered after her. "I see you're packing up. Are you planning to keep this place?"

"I haven't decided."

Esther stopped at the door. "I hope you will. The apple never falls far from the tree, so I'd enjoy having you next door."

After the woman left, Morgan leaned against the door to catch her breath. She was still recovering from the fright of Esther's unexpected arrival and the onslaught of desire Josh's proximity had elicited.

In the study, the closet bi-folds creaked, and in seconds Josh joined her in the hall. "She's gone?"

"Why didn't you come out? I would have introduced you."

He avoided her gaze, and when he spoke, he sounded too casual. "My appearance would have only complicated things. Esther might have stayed longer."

"You know her?"

"We met a couple of times when I visited Frank. She was constantly bringing a batch of fresh cookies or a loaf of homemade bread, which your dad always ate, and then he had to play twice as much racquetball to keep his weight down."

His reply was relaxed and easy, but his eyes were shuttered like a house in a storm. The uncomfortable notion that he hadn't wanted Mrs. Clark to see him niggled at her, reinforcing her previous suspicions.

"Ready to finish packing?" he asked.

"In a minute."

Josh returned to the study, and she entered the kitchen. When she'd believed Lashner's man had arrived, fear had parched her mouth, and she longed for something cool and wet to wash away the sensation of spiderwebs in her throat. She reached into a top cabinet for a glass, and her gaze fell on the counter of the pass-through.

"Josh!"

He appeared almost instantly. "What is it?"

"The one place we forgot to look."

She pointed to the answering machine, half hidden on the countertop by the drooping fronds of the fern. Its blinking red digits indicated two calls.

Josh punched the rewind button, then play. A computerized voice announced the date and time.

"That's the day Dad died," Morgan cried.

"Frank," a man's voice said, "this is Rob—"

"It's Lashner." Josh's face turned cold with fury.

"Meet me at the plant at seven tonight, in your lab. I want to discuss that offer of mine you've been resisting."

Josh stabbed the stop button with such force, the machine jumped.

"That's proof, isn't it?" Morgan said. "Lashner lured Dad there to kill him."

Josh shook his head. "It's not enough. It only explains why your father was at the plant that night. We still can't prove the explosion wasn't accidental."

"But if we do—"

"Then this could be another nail in Lashner's coffin." Josh flipped open the machine and reached for the tape.

"What about the second message?"

Josh closed the lid and pressed play again. The automated voice announced the current date and a time just a few hours earlier that afternoon.

Then the same male voice filled the room. "Morgan, this is Robert Lashner. We met briefly at your father's funeral. I'm assuming you're staying at Frank's place. I've been meaning to invite you to dinner, my dear, so we can share our memories of Frank.''

Morgan frowned as the smooth, cool voice left a number at which he could be reached. The tall, pencil-slim man with coiffed gray hair and mustache and wearing a European hand-tailored suit had shaken her hand solemnly at her father's graveside and shed crocodile tears into a black silk handkerchief.

So refined and civilized with impeccable manners. Who would have believed he had tried twice to have her killed?

Who would have believed he'd murdered her father, a doting and loving parent, a considerate neighbor, a brilliant chemist, a good friend? Frank Winters hadn't deserved to have his life snuffed out simply because he was an impediment to Robert Lashner's greed.

Her determination hardened like steel, and she curled her fists at her sides.

"Whatever it takes," she reiterated to Josh, "tell me, and I'll do it. I want that—" she struggled for a word vile enough to describe Lashner, but couldn't find it "—that sorry excuse for a human being to pay for what he's done."

She looked up into the deep richness of Josh's brown eyes and met agreement. Josh ejected the tape and slid it into his jacket pocket.

"Should I return his call?" Morgan asked. "Maybe if I have dinner with him, he'll make a slip, say something to incriminate himself."

"Lashner's too smart for that. He's only inviting you to draw you out so his thugs can grab you. He probably called because his men reported they'd lost you at the airport.''

"I thought that's what you wanted, to use me as bait.''

Guilt flickered across the strong planes of his face. "But not to put you in real danger. Ben and I are working on a plan, one that will force Lashner's hand.''

"And it involves me?'' She ached for a chance to insure Lashner's punishment.

"You bet.'' The set of his jaw and the hard look in Josh's eyes mirrored her resolve. "Together, we'll bring Robert Lashner down.''

MORGAN SPENT the following morning delving into the photograph albums, journals and letters she had brought back to Ben's from her father's condo. The process brought cleansing tears that lightened her grief and made her feel she had enjoyed one last visit with her father, whom she'd lost in such a cruel and senseless way.

She found nothing to incriminate Robert Lashner, but something else she didn't find disturbed her more.

She had scanned every journal from the year her father moved to Florida through the past year. His entries solidly confirmed his friendship with Ben Wells, his dislike and distrust of Robert Lashner, and his fondness for Esther Clark, his doting, elderly neighbor.

Not a single line contained Josh's name or any reference to him.

At a polished mahogany table built for twenty, she

ate a lonely luncheon in the dining room with its wraparound view of the gulf and pondered the significance of Josh's absence from her father's recollections. Josh's accounts of his years as her father's friend had been convincing, but, according to the journals, Josh's stories had all been lies.

If he'd lied about his friendship with her dad, what else had he lied about?

The dilemma stole her appetite, and she pushed away the Wedgwood china plate, her salad of chicken and Tokay grapes barely touched. Ben would have the solution to this puzzle, and he was returning home from the hospital this afternoon.

She and her questions would be waiting for him.

After lunch, she lingered in the living room, browsing through magazines without really seeing them. When the grandfather clock against the stairwell in the foyer chimed twice in the stillness, she began to pace the entry hall, listening for the hum of tires on the sweeping brick drive. At their arrival, she flung open the double doors and rushed out into the torrid sunshine of the Florida afternoon.

Harper had parked the dark blue limo close to the front door and removed a folding wheelchair from the trunk. He extended the chair, secured its braces and opened the rear door. Morgan watched with a catch in her throat while he assisted Ben from the car to the chair, attached a small oxygen canister to the rear of the chair and rolled Ben toward her.

"Welcome home." Her rush of affection at the sight of him surprised her.

Ben lifted his face and took her hand in his gauze-covered ones. The ubiquitous bandages swathed his features, his dark glasses protected his damaged eyes, and the oxygen mask covered his nose and mouth. She had to bend closer to hear his reply.

"It's good to be home, and especially to have you waiting. When you left for the airport the other night, I wasn't sure I'd see you again."

"I'm back safe and sound, thanks to you."

"And thanks to Josh." He squeezed her hand gently before releasing it, and Harper wheeled him into the house.

She followed them into the living room. Harper parked Ben's chair beside a low table and pulled the draperies against the bright glare of the sun.

"Do you wish the lights on, sir?" he asked.

Ben looked to Morgan. "It's up to you."

The closed curtains had plunged the room into dusky shadows, but she considered Ben's impaired eyes and shook her head.

"Thanks, Harper. That will be all." The oxygen mask distorted Ben's voice but didn't totally obliterate its pleasant resonance.

The stocky manservant withdrew, and Morgan dragged a chintz-upholstered hassock beside Ben's chair and sat at his feet.

"Now," he said, "tell me everything, starting with the last time I saw you."

Morgan launched into her tale, beginning with the attempted kidnapping. The clock in the foyer was striking three when she related the discovery of Lashner's messages on her father's answering machine.

Ben's attentive listening, broken only by an occasional brief question, put her at ease, and she savored the relaxing comfort of his company.

Unlike Josh.

When the private investigator had drawn her close in the study closet last night, she had been anything but comfortable. In spite of her fear, her blood had run hot at the sensation of his hard chest beneath her cheek. Her body had reacted as if Josh possessed some mysterious power to stimulate her senses and stir her blood. And all the while her mind shouted that she shouldn't, couldn't, trust a man who carried so many secrets.

Ben's company was a soothing contrast. With him, her hormones didn't riot, and her fears subsided in the presence of his affection and respect. She had trusted him instinctively from the moment they met, and the entries in her father's journals had assured her that trust was well-founded.

Ben's voice shattered her thoughts. "I knew this charade wasn't going to be easy for you."

"The hardest part," she said, "is trusting Josh. If you didn't constantly assure me he's trustworthy, I wouldn't have anything to do with him."

"Why not?" Surprise and concern tinged Ben's question.

"There's something elusive about him I can't put my finger on." No need to bother Ben with the unsettling effect his investigator had on her. "And he doesn't always tell the truth."

His tone hardened. "He's lied to you?"

Taking time to phrase her answer, she combed her fingers through her hair and tucked it behind her ears. Josh had said Ben didn't trust easily, but obviously Ben trusted Josh. Josh was Ben's friend, after all, so she had better tread carefully.

"He claims he was Dad's friend, but he isn't mentioned in Dad's journals."

Ben expelled a long sigh, as if he'd been holding his breath. "Josh's work is delicate and secretive. What makes him an efficient investigator and also keeps him alive is his anonymity. That's why he prefers to work at night, why I haven't told you his last name. His few close friends are aware of Josh's need for obscurity. That's why your father never wrote about him. For Josh's protection."

His explanation did little to allay her supicion. Her father surely would have referred somehow to Josh, if only as an anonymous friend, in the accounts of his daily life, but Ben seemed unperturbed.

Maybe she was imagining problems where none existed. Admittedly, she was under a lot of stress, and her mistrust and apprehension were based more on intuition than concrete evidence.

She shivered, recalling Josh's embrace. The fact that when she was close to him, she didn't trust herself, much less him, added to her uneasiness.

"You will keep working with him, won't you?" Ben asked.

She attempted a smile. "I suppose I have to if I want to avenge my father's murder."

"Your association with Josh involves more than bringing Lashner to justice. As the attack at the airport proves, you also need Josh to keep you alive."

She nodded, contrite that Ben had done so much in his efforts to protect her, yet she couldn't bring herself to trust the man he had chosen to keep her safe. "I'll do whatever it takes to see this through."

"You're the bravest woman I know."

He caressed her cheek with his bandaged hand, and she leaned into his gentle touch.

"Is it bravery," she asked, "when you haven't got a choice?"

"You always have a choice, Morgan. I can send you out of the country until Lashner is exposed, or—"

"No." She covered his hand with her own. "I'll see this through. For both our sakes. And especially for my father."

He reached into the pocket of his jacket, withdrew a folded paper and handed it to her. "You'll need this."

"What is it?"

"The proxy you gave me." He withdrew his hand from hers. "It's time to flush Lashner out. As chairman of the board at Chemco, I've called a meeting for two weeks from today."

"Will you be strong enough to attend?"

"My doctor says yes, but I've had my secretary tell the board members I may not be there. Lashner can't take the chance of you or me appearing at that meeting and defeating his motion to sell Frank's miracle formula. He'll have to make a move soon. When he does, we'll be ready."

Harper announced his presence in the doorway with a discreet clearing of his throat. "Mr. Josh is on the telephone, sir."

"I'll take the call in my bedroom," Ben said.

"Shall I wait?" Morgan asked.

"I won't be long. When I return, we'll decide on our next step."

Fear twisted through her like a corkscrew of black ice, and her anxiety must have registered on her face.

"You mustn't worry," Ben said. "I promised your father I would keep you safe, and I always keep my promises."

Harper rolled Ben into his bedroom, and she stared at the heavy door as it closed behind him. Ben had vowed to keep her safe, but the execution of that vow depended on Josh. Only time would tell if she could trust him to keep Ben's promises.

And keep her alive.

JOSH LOUNGED AGAINST the weathered railing of the boardwalk over the sand dunes and observed the house. A light shone behind the draperies in Morgan's bedroom window, visible above the vine-covered wall that surrounded the estate. As he watched, the light blinked out.

She would be coming soon now.

Turning back toward the gulf, he lifted his face into the onshore breeze, inhaling the tang of salt and the scent of elusive freedom. He steeled himself against his first glimpse of her, so his face wouldn't give him away. More than anything, he longed to scoop her into his arms as soon as she appeared, but such behavior would be disastrous. To keep her safe, as he'd promised, he had to remain aloof and wary.

One slip could mean her death.

Dear God, he was tired. An overwhelming longing to chuck it all, the lurking in shadows, the devious-ness, the lies, gripped him.

Just a few more days, two weeks at most, he promised himself. By then Lashner would be behind bars. Morgan would be safe.

And Josh could disappear.

He felt her presence before he saw her. The rhythmic beat of her footsteps vibrated through the boards at his feet. Turning toward the house, he watched her approach like a dream in the night. Jeans sheathed her slender legs. A fitted jacket nipped her tiny waist, and a dark navy scarf, its ends fluttering in the wind, hid her fair hair.

When she reached him, moonlight sparkled in her eyes and illuminated the rosy glow of her cheeks. If he hadn't known better, he would have thought she was glad to see him.

Fat chance.

She had told Ben she didn't trust him. No, the flush on her face and the shimmer in her eyes were caused only by the cool night air and impending danger.

He slammed a lid on the surge of joy and desire at her arrival. "All set?"

She halted abruptly, taken aback by his bluntness. "And a good evening to you, too."

"Time's running out. Small talk's a waste of it."

His frustration had sharpened his temper, and she cringed visibly at his harshness. He couldn't reveal the source of his foul humor, because then she'd trust him even less, knowing how much he wanted her.

But he could apologize. "Sorry. I didn't mean to snap."

Her forgiving smile almost undid him.

"I understand. I was feeling tense and nervous, too, until I crossed the dunes." She hopped off the steps onto the sand, spread her arms and pirouetted in the moonlight, as light and graceful as a dancer. "Isn't it a marvelous night?"

"Morgan."

The annoyance in his voice stopped her. "I know, I'm wasting time. Which way?"

He pointed south toward the distant city and ambled down to the hard-packed sand of the high-tide line. She fell in step beside him, and the salt breeze now carried a hint of her perfume.

"Did you call your dad's secretary?" he asked.

"I told Brenda I'd come to the plant sometime later this evening to clear out Dad's office."

"Good. Then it's all arranged."

"It took some persuading. She insisted I come during the day, but I said I couldn't deal with the condolences of Dad's co-workers right now."

Her voice came in breathless huffs, and he slowed his steps to ease her pace. "Do you have your father's office keys?"

"The funeral director gave them to me, along with Dad's wallet and other personal effects, before the service. Brenda said she would alert the night watchman to let me in at the main gate."

"Let's hope this works," he muttered to himself.

Morgan stopped suddenly and tugged on his arm. "How can you be certain Lashner will know I'm coming?"

With her head thrown back to gaze up at him and small hands pushed into her pockets, *ethereal* and *vulnerable* sprang again to his mind. But her fragility was only an illusion. Any woman gutsy enough to walk knowingly into a trap in order to snare the trapper had to have a backbone of case-hardened steel.

"Lashner," he said, "had a man waiting at the airport and people all over town searching for you. If I've guessed right, he also instructed Brenda Jernigan to tell him immediately if you contacted her."

"So he'll be waiting." She sounded resigned but unafraid, and his heart swelled at her courage.

"He or one of his goons. Either way, I'm prepared. Now, let's get moving or we'll be late."

"I didn't tell Brenda a specific time."

"I didn't mean late to the plant. We're meeting someone on the edge of town in fifteen minutes."

She picked up her pace without questions, and he repressed a self-satisfied smile. Okay, so she didn't trust him, but at least she'd agreed to his plans with an implied recognition that he would enlighten her when she needed to know.

The stretch of private beach in front of waterfront mansions gave way to deserted public beaches. Within minutes, Josh, with Morgan in tow, trudged across a wide strip of sand toward an old-fashioned diner, the lone building in the empty landscape.

"You're going inside without a disguise?" Morgan asked.

"You'll see."

He skirted the bright glare of the partially filled parking lot until he reached the far corner where a light was burned out. A dilapidated panel van with a surfboard lashed to the roof, its front seat empty, was parked in the shadows.

Josh approached the van and rapped once, then twice, on its right side. Immediately its door slid open, and Josh lifted Morgan inside. The door slammed shut behind them.

Even though he knew what to expect, the van's interior astounded him. The walls, banked with electronic equipment, looked like a miniversion of NASA's mission control.

A young man in a swivel chair pivoted from a wall of toggle switches, dials and flickering lights to face them. "You're right on time."

Josh savored Morgan's openmouthed expression of surprise. "Morgan, Sal Oliveri. Sal, meet Morgan."

Sal, the epitome of Italian good looks and charm, hoisted himself from his chair and offered the seat to Morgan. She gave him a cursory nod, sank into the chair and gazed in amazement at the paraphernalia surrounding her.

"What is all this?" she asked.

"Surveillance equipment," Sal said. "I'm a private investigator, and this stuff comes in handy in my line of work. Would you like a demonstration?"

Morgan nodded.

Sal adjusted a few dials and flipped on a speaker. The clatter of dishes, the sizzle of a grill and a jumble of voices filled the van. "Those sounds are coming from the diner, almost a hundred yards from here."

"That's amazing," Morgan said with awe.

Sal's dark eyes flashed, and his wide grin deepened the cleft in his chin. "Baby, you ain't seen nothing yet."

With a few adjustments, the jumble of voices narrowed until one customer's voice sounded loud and clear, placing an order for a medium-rare burger and a chocolate shake. The waitress's bored query about french fries was equally intelligible.

Josh knelt on the van floor and leaned against the closed door, enjoying Morgan's unmistakable fascination with Sal's electronic gadgetry. Her eyes, just a shade lighter than her navy scarf, shimmered with the excitement of a child's at Christmas.

"What did you do," she asked, "plant microphones in the diner?"

"No need," Sal explained, "Directional mikes pick up the voices from here."

She turned to Josh. "Are we here for directional mikes?"

"Not exactly," he said. "What have you got for me, Sal?"

Sal opened a cabinet beneath his computer keyboard and dragged out an aluminum carrier, smaller than a piece of luggage, but larger than an attaché case. "Here's everything you need."

Sal slid him the case, which he accepted without opening. If Sal said everything was there, it was all there. He'd dealt with the Tampa-based investigator often enough to trust him without question.

Rising to his feet, Josh picked up the case. "Looks like it's show time."

Morgan stood also. "I'm ready."

"You know where to send the bill," Josh told his friend.

"Gotcha." Sal flashed a grin and extended his hand to Morgan. "I'd be worried about you if I didn't know my buddy here will guard you with his life. Do what he says, and you'll be fine."

"Thanks." Morgan shook his hand, slipped out

the door Sal opened and stared across the lot toward the diner.

In the doorway, Josh turned to Sal and lowered his voice. "What about the other?"

Sal lifted a small canister from a nearby shelf. "Be careful with this stuff. It can be dangerous."

Josh slipped the container into his jacket pocket and left the van. The door slammed behind him, and in seconds the engine sputtered to life and the vehicle pulled away.

Josh gripped the cold surface of the canister in his pocket. Dangerous, Sal had called it.

If it was needed, Josh hoped it would be lethal.

Chapter Six

Shaking her head in amazement, Morgan watched Sal's van disappear in a cloud of sand along the beach access road.

"That's unbelievable equipment," she said. "Without it, the only audible sound from the diner is the thump of the bass from the sound system."

Josh grasped her arm and pulled her deeper into the shadows toward his car, parked next to where the van had been.

"I left the car here earlier," he said. "Get in."

She climbed in the front seat, and he circled around, scooted behind the wheel and wedged the aluminum case on the seat between them.

"Take off your jacket," he said.

Recalling the car's inadequate air-conditioning, she shrugged out of her jacket, folded it neatly and laid it across the back of the seat.

"Now your blouse."

"What?" Thinking she'd misunderstood, she peered through the darkness to read his expression, but his face was obscured by shadows.

"It's dark," he said in a strangely uninflected

tone, as if fighting to keep his voice calm. "No one will see."

"I've done some crazy things in my day," she admitted as heat rose from her neck to her forehead, "but stripping in public isn't one of them. And I don't intend to now."

"This isn't public. Just take off the blouse."

The flatness in his voice was beginning to annoy her. "You must have a reason for such a request. Would you mind explaining?"

"Don't make this any harder than it already is," he snapped.

She curbed her rising distrust. "Tell me what you're planning."

He leaned away from her with a painful sigh, and the dim light from the parking lot silhouetted his striking profile against the window. "I can't accompany you into the plant or I may scare off Lashner's goons. If I send you in wearing a wire—"

"A wire?"

"A microphone. So I can monitor what's going on."

She exhaled with embarrassment and relief. For a moment, imagining he'd transformed into a sex-starved Romeo eager for necking in the parked car, she feared she had unwittingly relayed signals of her undeniable attraction to him.

She should have known better. Josh was one cool customer, not likely to indulge in playing around on the job or to attribute any significance to tiny, involuntary signs she couldn't control.

Her relief was short-lived.

If Josh wasn't yet aware of how he affected her,

he would have little doubt if she removed her clothes. She clutched her blouse and pulled the collar closed at the neckline. Her heart was palpitating more forcefully than the thumping bass that rocked the distant diner.

"Just attach the mike to my blouse," she said, "and I'll cover it with my jacket."

"We can't chance someone discovering and disabling it, just when you might need it most," he said with irritating common sense.

Either emotion had caused a catch in his voice or she was imagining things again, projecting her own uncontrollable responses onto him. Whichever the case, delaying wouldn't resolve her dilemma. If they were to set their trap for Lashner, she had to follow Josh's instructions.

Attempting nonchalance, she tugged her shirt from her jeans and undid the buttons, silently cursing her clumsy, shaking fingers. She slipped her arms from the sleeves and left the garment draped over her shoulders.

Josh flipped the catches on the case, lifted the lid and extracted a small round object, no bigger than a berry, with a trailing wire. He removed a roll of tape, laid the objects on the dashboard and shifted the case to the back seat. When he slid into the space where the case had been, his body heat seared her side.

"Now your bra." His eyes glittered in the darkness and his warm breath raised goose bumps on her faintly chilled skin.

She inhaled the stirring masculinity of his scent, and her pulse galloped. "Is this really necessary?"

"The safest place to hide the mike is between your

breasts." A hoarseness in his voice betrayed his apparent calm.

She fumbled to open the front clasp of her bra. The sooner she could dress again, the better. Her reactions were too dangerous, too certain to create trouble if she didn't squelch them.

Josh's fingers skimmed the cleft between her breasts as he secured the tiny microphone with medical adhesive tape he had ripped off the roll with his teeth. The trembling of his fingers shot a sympathetic vibration through her.

She closed her eyes in an ineffective attempt to subdue her defiant senses. Although no man had ever affected her this intensely, her response *had* to be reflexive. How could she care for a man she didn't really know or fully trust?

More gooseflesh erupted when he trailed the attached wire down her midriff to her waist and taped it. More than a foot of wire still dangled loose. He drew back, his breathing as tortured as if he'd run a marathon.

"What do I do with the rest of this antenna?" she asked, already guessing the answer.

"We'll have to snake it inside your jeans."

Afraid of losing all control if he touched her again, she hastily unzipped her jeans, lifted her hips and thrust the wire across her abdomen and down her left leg. With equally rapid movements, she fastened her bra and jeans and shoved her arms into her blouse.

"Morgan."

The tender resonance of her name on his lips pierced her with a longing as acute as an illness. To escape the exquisite torture, she wrenched open the door and fled from the car to the shadows of a nearby dune. Stuffing her shirttail back into her jeans, she breathed deeply and tried to regain command of her mutinous heart and steady her quivering body.

She'd read somewhere that danger was an aphrodisiac. If so, she rationalized, the peril of her situation, not Josh, produced her passionate responses.

Right, a mocking inner voice taunted, *and pigs fly.*

She shivered in the onshore breeze, then jumped in surprise when Josh, whose approach she hadn't heard, draped her jacket over her shoulders.

"Sorry if I embarrassed you." His attitude was all business. "The wire had to be placed."

"You're right. I'm just nervous," she lied, and slid her arms into her jacket.

"Let's go where there's more light."

She walked beside him back to the parking lot and stopped beneath the glow of a low-sodium light. He grasped her shoulders and turned her in one direction, then another as he stared at her chest.

"The wire's completely hidden," he said. "Now we have to test it."

"How?"

He reached into his back pocket for his wallet and extracted a few bills. "Walk over to the diner and order a couple of coffees to go. I can test the equipment and its range, and we can use the caffeine. It's going to be a long night."

She took the bills and strode toward the diner until a worry pulled her up short. She turned back to Josh. "I'm not in disguise."

"I doubt Lashner has anyone staking out the Gulfside Grill.'' He gave her a thumbs-up, a heart-melting smile and headed back to his car.

The closer to the diner she advanced, the more her reaction to Josh troubled her. She had always believed she'd have to love a man before he could turn her on like Josh had. But what was there to love about him, a man she barely knew?

Her perfidious mind obligingly ticked off the points. His drop-dead gorgeous smile, a physique that turned women's heads, his willingness to risk his life for her, his loyalty to Ben, the tender way he eased her anxiety—

Stop it!

For a moment she feared she had spoken aloud and the mike between her breasts had transmitted her words. She'd have a hard time explaining her exclamation.

She was Ben's wife, she reminded herself. She owed her loyalty, affection and any explanations to him. Josh was only an investigator and bodyguard, and that's all he would ever be.

Confident the brisk walk and cool air had cleared both body and mind of foolish notions, she jerked open the door of the Gulfside Grill and went inside.

A blast of steamy air, laden with odors of cooking grease, cigarette smoke and too many bodies assailed her, and the bright blaze of fluorescent lights hurt her eyes. From one corner, a Wurlitzer jukebox blasted out a country-western ballad. She spied an empty stool at the far end of the crowded counter and headed for it, avoiding eye contact with the customers.

She settled onto the seat. A rail-thin waitress, her

dingy white uniform brightened by a garish pink handkerchief pinned to her bodice like a corsage, took her order with a bored sigh and moved away.

The mike burned against Morgan's skin and felt the size of a grapefruit. She pictured a neon sign above her flashing She's Wearing a Wire, with an arrow pointed at the top of her head. The ridiculous image made her smile and calmed her shaky nerves.

"You sure have got a purty grin, darlin'." A man on her left swiveled his stool toward her. "Don't I know you from somewhere?"

She glanced quickly at the beefy frame and lumpy, sunburned face of the stranger who'd just tossed her the oldest line in the book. "No."

Leaning forward and away from him, she peered behind the counter, where her waitress, empty cups in hand, gabbed with the short-order cook. Morgan drummed her fingertips impatiently on the Formica surface. She would wait another minute, then leave. Josh should have heard enough by now to test his equipment.

"You're not very friendly." Undeterred, the man at her side bent closer and ran his finger down her arm. "Think you're too good for me, do you?"

Cringing at his touch, she jerked away and grimaced at the stink of onions on his breath, but she said nothing. A reply would only encourage him.

He edged nearer, so close his thick lips brushed her hair. "You and me could have us a real good time, darlin'. There's a place up the road we could get a few beers, have a few dances. After that, who knows?"

She recoiled from his suggestive laugh. The waitress still chattered with the cook, so Morgan hopped from the stool and headed toward the door.

She had gone only a few feet when a rough hand grabbed her elbow, lifting her until her feet barely touched the floor.

"Keep moving, darlin'," the stranger's voice rumbled in her ear. "We'll find my pick'em-up truck and see if I can't thaw you out a bit. Make you a lot more friendly, if you know what I mean."

Morgan attempted to shake off his grasp.

"I'm not going anywhere with you. Take your hands off me," she said in a low but steady voice. The last thing she wanted was to attract attention.

The obnoxious man either didn't hear or didn't care. Before she could protest further, he had yanked her through the door and shoved her into the parking lot.

"Let me go!" She was struggling to wrest away, when the possibility the man wasn't what he seemed struck terror through her. "You're working for Lashner, aren't you?"

"Honey, I don't know nobody named Lashner. I don't work for nobody but me. Tonight I'm taking time off for fun. And you're gonna provide it."

"Sure about that, are you?" Josh's deep voice rang out in the stillness of the parking lot.

He stood just a few feet away, blocking the big stranger's path. Josh's stance was relaxed and easy, and the expression on his face benign.

"Back off, pal." The man tightened his grip on her arm. "I saw her first."

"Hey, good buddy," Josh said, mimicking the man's folksy speech, "sorry to disappoint you, but

I've got three good reasons why the lady can't go with you.''

"Yeah? Like what?'' Her captor staggered, slightly drunk. Onions had masked the liquor on his breath.

"For starters—'' Josh ambled closer "—she doesn't want to go with you.''

"Shucks,'' the big man said, "a few minutes alone with me in my truck, and I'll change her mind.''

Morgan jerked her arm, but couldn't free herself from the stranger's grasp.

"Second—'' Josh flashed her a warning look and kept coming closer "—she's married to me.''

Morgan's eyes widened and her jaw dropped at the lie.

The man grabbed her left hand. "Then why ain't she wearing a ring?''

"Sweetheart—'' Josh shot her a rebuking look "—how many times have I said you're asking for trouble when you leave your wedding band at home?''

Still gaping at Josh's bizarre behavior, Morgan didn't respond.

Josh advanced within arm's reach. His genial facade didn't alter, and seemingly unruffled, he rocked easily from his heels to the balls of his feet with his hands shoved in the back pockets of his jeans.

What game was he playing?

The man dragged her closer. "That's only two reasons. The third better be good, 'cause I ain't heard nothing yet to change my mind.''

When Josh grinned, a dangerous light flickered in

his dark eyes, and she read what he'd managed to hide until now.

The clod who held her had to be crazy as well as drunk. Was he blind to the coiled strength in Josh's broad shoulders and muscled arms, the heightened alertness of his long, powerful legs, his weight balanced on the balls of his feet, ready to spring, and the killer glare behind the friendly cast of his brown eyes?

Josh pulled his hands from his pockets and dropped them at his sides. "The third reason's too good to waste if I don't have to. Just let the lady go."

The beefy man snorted like an enraged bull and turned away, hauling Morgan with him.

Josh lunged and clamped the man's shoulder in a steel grip. "Hey, good buddy. You can't leave yet. I haven't told you the third reason."

"Huh?" Groggy from drink, the man turned back toward Josh. "Okay, give it to me, so I can get on with my fun."

"You're sure?"

Thinking she'd imagined Josh's leashed threat, Morgan bit back her disgust and twisted in the man's drunken grip. If Josh were any friendlier with the old coot, the pair would soon be slow-dancing in the parking lot.

"Yeah," the man said, "show me."

Josh shrugged. "Just remember, you asked for it."

In the blink of an eye, Josh's expression changed from genial to deadly. He raised his right hand, formed a massive fist and held it in front of the man's reddened nose. "*This* is the third reason."

Before the man could comprehend what was happening, Josh landed a jarring punch on her captor's jaw. The blow broke the man's hold on her, and he slid to the ground against a nearby car, out cold.

Dumbfounded, Morgan waited as Josh strode to the diner, opened the door and yelled, "Somebody call 911. A man's passed out in the parking lot."

He pivoted, loped back to her and grabbed her hand. "Let's get out of here."

When he broke into a run, she raced to keep up with him.

A few minutes later, she was safely ensconced in the dim interior of the Chevy next to Josh, who appeared as calm as if nothing had happened.

He wasn't even breathing hard.

"Thanks," she said after catching her breath. "Rescuing me is getting to be a habit with you."

"You're welcome." His grin thawed his usual aloofness. "Private Investigator Josh, at your service to fend off amorous drunks, deter kidnappers, slay dragons and hang the moon."

She nestled against the seat with a contented sigh.

Slay dragons and hang the moon?

She was beginning to believe he actually could.

JOSH WAITED for the hubbub outside the diner to die down. And for his furious blood to cool. As soon as he had picked up the old redneck's lecherous comments on the transmitter, he had sprinted to the diner, ready to tear the man limb from limb.

No longer could he kid himself that protecting Morgan Winters was just a job, an obligation he'd accepted on a friend's behalf. Keeping her safe had become his personal, private crusade.

And tonight, keeping her safe had just become a whole lot more complicated.

He had been a fool to expect he could touch the silky smoothness of her skin, skim the rounded contours of her breasts and the warm expanse of her midriff without being stirred. As much as he wanted to deny it, his reflex had been more than basic lust. Deep caring and respect undergirded his desire. He longed to worship her with his body.

That longing could get them both killed.

A lot of good his self-lecture earlier in the evening had done. If he didn't find some way to switch off his fascination with the incredibly brave, beautiful woman at his side, he would be useless in a crisis.

Even if his infatuation didn't impede his effectiveness, another major complication hindered any chance of involvement with her. In Morgan's eyes, Josh would be a first-class jerk if he encouraged her to reciprocate his feelings. Morgan was married to Ben.

Now there was a hell of a snafu.

She insisted the marriage was in name only, but he sensed her fondness for Ben and her reluctance to betray him in any way.

"What are we waiting for?" Morgan said.

What indeed? For two cents, he would abandon every principle and make love to her like a sex-starved teenager, right on the front seat. Defying a hunger that was almost agonizing, he scanned the distant diner and addressed the real intent of her question.

"We're waiting for the crowd to disperse. It shouldn't take long now. Don Juan de Bubba is conscious and someone's helping him inside."

She shivered, as if remembering the creep's advances. "I take it the mike works?"

"Loud and clear. And a good thing, too." He flashed her a teasing glance. "Unless you were looking forward to a tumble in the back of his pickup."

"You are so bad," she said in mock outrage.

As he had hoped, his joking made her smile and released the magnetic tension that sizzled between them in the warm intimacy of the Chevy.

A car, pulling out of the parking lot, swept her face with its headlights.

"Much better," Josh said. "Your color's coming back."

Her expression sobered. "The worst is still ahead."

"Right." He squelched his tenderness and returned to business. "All's clear at the diner. Let's walk, and I'll fill you in on the plan."

He climbed from the car, waited for her to join him, then crossed the dunes to smooth sands, damp from the ebbing tide. Together they strolled along the water's edge where a night heron squawked and skittered from their path, and the gentle splash of curling surf accompanied their steps. Velvet darkness surrounded them, alleviated only by myriad crystals of moonlight reflected on the waves.

"I can't stress too much," Josh said, "how dangerous going to the plant complex will be. If you want to back out now, I wouldn't blame you."

She shook her head. "All my life I've been afraid

of taking risks, like when I didn't move to Florida with Dad after high school. As a result, I've made some terrible mistakes.''

Her earnestness renewed his tenderness toward her. ''Maybe you're being too hard on yourself.''

''No. Just realistic. For instance, if I'd dared to come here with Dad, I could have spent more time with him.''

''You couldn't know your father would die so young,'' he said. ''Hindsight's always twenty-twenty.''

''True, but all my life I've taken the safe path— the secure but boring job, a bland but practical apartment, dull but dependable friends. I've avoided men who—''

She bit off the words as if she'd said too much, and trudged on, her hands thrust in her jacket pockets, her navy scarf billowing behind her in twin streamers. Her small sneakers left no indentations in the wet sand, as if she were a figment of his heated imagination instead of flesh and blood, a bewitching contradiction of substance and illusion.

She stopped suddenly and faced him. ''By playing it safe, I've led a boring life and accomplished nothing. There has to be more to living than that. If going to the plant tonight means I can bring Lashner to justice and stop the sale of that dangerous formula, maybe I'll make up for what I've failed to do in the past.''

Fervor laced her voice, but in spite of her ferocious declaration to wager on her future, she looked achingly uncertain. Unable to stop himself, he reached out, cradled her face in his hands and lowered his lips to hers.

She didn't withdraw. After an inhalation of surprise, she raised on tiptoe and returned the pressure of his lips. Her lips parted, deepening the kiss, and she tasted of salt and sweetness and all the best things that were missing in his lonely life. When she lifted her arms to his neck and twisted her fingers in his hair, he wondered if the same frenzied desire that smoldered in his gut was burning in hers.

Had he lost his mind?

He jerked away as if singed, having done the very thing he'd promised himself he wouldn't. He withdrew his untrustworthy hands from her face, rammed them into his pockets and set off down the beach.

Morgan followed, half running to keep up.

"Sorry," he said when she reached him. "That was a stupid thing to do."

"Should I take that as an insult?"

He couldn't tell if her breathlessness came from exertion or hurt. He longed to embrace her again, but didn't dare. As long as he kept his hands in his pockets and his feet moving, maybe he could keep his head straight, too.

"You're one distracting lady," he said with a flippancy he didn't feel. "Tonight I can't be distracted."

"Maybe you're the one who should learn to take risks." Her soft voice fired through him like a shot of whiskey effervescing in his veins, making him light-headed with desire.

"With another man's wife?" He was purposely glacial, distancing himself.

Her sharp intake of breath indicated he'd scored a hit.

"As for risks—" he thrust a barrier of cold, hard facts between them "—you'll be taking risk enough for both of us tonight. Lashner intends to kill you."

"*My husband,*" she threw back at him with feisty emphasis, "has hired you to make sure that doesn't happen."

Good. He had made her mad. Anger was easier to deal with than hurt. "I'll need your full cooperation."

"You'll have it. Just tell me what to do."

He took a deep breath. As long as he concentrated on the plan, he wouldn't do anything foolish, like kissing her again. "First, you'll search your father's office, just in case Lashner overlooked something important."

"Do you really think he's left anything incriminating for me to find?"

"Probably not. Ben had Harper search Lashner's office today—"

"Today? Why not weeks ago?" she asked.

"Today was Harper's first chance to sneak in without breaking locks and raising Lashner's suspicion that someone is on to him. Harper told Lashner's secretary that Ben needed a contract Lashner was working on." Josh's pulse rate eased as he focused on the task at hand and avoided the bright look in her eyes.

"Did Harper find anything?"

"If Lashner did keep anything significant there, he removed it after the explosion."

"So searching Dad's office is probably a waste of time, too." Resignation weighted her voice.

"It's crucial to the plan. When you visit the plant complex, you have to appear as if you're collecting your father's belongings. You can't tip off Lashner's men that clearing Frank's office isn't your reason for being there."

"While I'm in Dad's office seems like a perfect opportunity for someone to—" her voice faltered, and she straightened her shoulders and cleared her throat before continuing "—for someone to kill me."

He slowed his steps, but stopped himself from reaching out to her. "Lashner won't try anything in the plant complex. He can't risk a murder investigation at Chemco tainting his efforts to sell the formula. Much better for him if you simply disappear."

"If there's nothing in Dad's office and Lashner's men won't make their move in the plant, why am I going there?"

"To flush out his accomplices without giving away your hiding place at Ben's." Outlining the details of the scheme to trap Frank Winters's killer made it easier to suppress his need, but fear for her replaced his longing. "We must assume Lashner will have a man waiting at or near the plant, ready to follow as soon as you leave. Once you're far enough away from Chemco, he'll probably grab you, first chance he gets."

"Not if you're with me."

"I won't be." He grasped her arm, pivoting her back in the direction of the diner.

"Why not?" Her voice was sharp with alarm. She

stopped and dug her heels into the sand. "Aren't you supposed to be protecting me?"

"We'll take separate cars. If they see you with me, they'll sense a trap. There's a rental car parked beside my Chevy in the diner lot. You'll drive it, and I'll follow at a safe distance. I've arranged for Jim Dexter, an ex-policeman friend of mine, to wait near the plant as backup."

She scrunched her face in concentration. "So you believe Lashner's men won't approach me until after I've left the plant complex?"

"I'm assuming—hoping they'll pick up your trail there, then follow to discover where you're staying."

"But I'm staying at Ben's. I can't lead them there."

He shook his head. "I've rented adjoining rooms at a nearby motel, one for you, the other where Jim Dexter and I will wait. When Lashner's men make their move, we'll grab them."

"What if they reach me before you do?"

Her voice held no fear, but she seemed so petite, so exposed, his heart lurched with apprehension. He dug into the pocket of his jacket and withdrew the metal canister Sal had given him. "Carry this where you can reach it quickly."

She accepted the cylinder without hesitation and hefted it in her small hand. "Mace?"

"Pepper spray. If they close in, blast their faces. The spray's effects will immobilize them until I arrive."

He started to remind her to remain upwind of the spray so she wouldn't be affected, but he feared the extra instruction might slow her response. Pepper spray was disabling, but only rarely fatal. He'd rather take the chance of her receiving a nasty dose than dying at the hands of Lashner's thugs.

She rewarded him with beaming admiration. "You think of everything, don't you?"

God, I hope so.

"Just follow my directions," he said, "and you'll be fine."

Chapter Seven

Morgan drove the rented Lexus to the gatehouse at the Chemco Industries complex and handed her driver's license to the security guard.

A thin young man in a neatly pressed uniform studied her name and picture. "You're Frank Winters's daughter?"

"I'm here to clean out his office."

He bent down until his friendly face was level with her car window. "Your father was well liked by everyone, miss. If you need a hand with anything, just call security. We'll send someone right away."

In the control center behind him, an array of video monitors displayed rooms and exteriors of buildings throughout the plant. Knowing her movements inside the complex would be reflected on those screens bolstered her courage. The guard's watchfulness made a surprise attack by Lashner's men inside the plant unlikely, just as Josh had assured her.

"Thank you," Morgan said. "Everyone's been very kind."

He straightened, returned her license and, reaching

inside the control center, hit a lever that opened the steel gates to the grounds of the plant.

Casting a nervous glance at the rearview mirror, she drove through. Moments ago, when she had turned off the highway into the industrial park where Chemco was located, she had lost sight of Josh, who had been trailing her in his car. To pick up her voice, he had to be somewhere nearby. The transmitter range of the mike she wore was only a half mile or less, unless she remained out in the open.

The medical tape adhering the wire to her body itched against her skin, reminding her of Josh's warm hands and the agonizing pleasure of his touch. Her lips tingled with the memory of his kiss, tantalizing and forbidden. As unforgettable and thrilling as it had been, she wouldn't kiss him again.

Kissing him was too dangerous.

She had professed a willingness to take risks, but giving in to her attraction to Josh was a gamble she wasn't prepared to take. For every fragment of information she gleaned about him, contradictions arose. She must trust him to protect her, as Ben had hired him to do.

But she refused to trust him with her heart.

On the beach, when Josh had kissed her so unexpectedly and tenderly, she had responded with wanton desire. But just because her body betrayed her didn't mean her common sense had deserted her. If she ever gave her heart, it would be to a man like Ben Wells, gentle and kind and dependable, a man she could rely on to be who and what he said he was.

Maybe a relationship with Ben wouldn't produce the skyrocketing excitement she felt with Josh, but alone in the world with her father gone, she needed a man she could count on, a man with no secrets.

Josh whatever-his-last-name-was was full of secrets. She had seen them, lurking in the beguiling depths of his disarming brown eyes.

Tonight, after Josh had caught one of Lashner's men and turned him over to the police, she would never have to see Josh again.

Temptation would depart with him.

Even more important, her father's killer would be brought to justice and the dangers of the gasoline substitute exposed. Then she could settle down to a quiet and peaceful existence.

If she was lucky, Ben wouldn't want their marriage annulled, and she could devote herself to caring for her invalid husband. After all, he seemed to enjoy her company and had encouraged her to consider his home her own.

So you'll risk your life, but not your heart? an inner voice scoffed. *Where's your real courage?*

"Shut up!" she snapped aloud, and hoped Josh hadn't turned on his receiver.

At the administration building, she parked in the reserved space still marked with her father's name and locked the car. A light wind carried the lingering stench of ashes from the scarred earth across the street where demolition crews had scraped clean every vestige of the laboratory facility. Lashner had wasted no time in destroying any evidence the arson investigators might have missed.

She turned her back on the place where her father had died and headed up the wide walkway toward the entrance. Lights blazed in several offices as cleaning crews performed their nightly rounds. She discovered the entry doors unlocked, probably for the custodians.

In the dimly lit lobby, Morgan entered the elevator and poked the button for the third floor. Her last visit to her father's office had been at Christmas, when she had dragged him away for lunch. Her dad had loved his work so much, he had to be reminded to eat.

Anger toward Lashner overrode her grief and trampled her fears. He had struck down her father in the prime of his life, and she could not allow Lashner to go unpunished.

Her heart vaulted into her throat when the elevator stopped on the second floor. Josh had insisted she'd be safe inside the plant, but she didn't feel safe. She felt alone and exposed. She should have taken the stairs, but she'd been so obsessed with castigating Lashner, she hadn't considered his men might trap her in the elevator.

She held her breath as the doors slid open.

A heavy-set woman in a polyester uniform with Sunshine Custodial Service stitched above the breast pocket was dumping plastic bags of trash into a receptacle on a cleaning cart and whistling an off-key tune.

At the sight of her, Morgan relaxed, then tensed again as she realized a woman who could be carrying a gun would be as dangerous as any man. She slipped her hand into her jacket pocket and gripped the cool, reassuring metal of the pepper spray canister.

"Didn't know anyone was working tonight except

us,'' the cleaning woman said pleasantly and dragged her cart onto the elevator.

Before the doors could close, Morgan slipped off. Watching the illuminated indicator above the door, she waited until the elevator stopped at the third floor and continued to the fifth before she took the stairs. At the third-floor stairwell's glass-paneled door, she paused and scanned the empty hallway. If the cleaning woman had exited the elevator on this floor, she must have entered one of the offices.

Morgan burst from the stairwell entry and scooted across the hallway to her father's office. She was reaching in her pocket for his keys when she noticed the strip of bright light beneath the door.

Someone was inside.

Her instincts said run, until she remembered the mike that connected her to Josh and security's high-tech surveillance cameras. She'd have help in minutes if she needed it. With the pepper spray firmly in one hand, she tried the door with the other. It was unlocked. She pushed the door open, prepared to fight or flee.

"Hello, Morgan, I was waiting for you." Brenda Jernigan, her father's longtime secretary, sat at her desk and welcomed Morgan with a too-bright smile.

Weak-kneed with relief, Morgan stuffed the aerosol can into her pocket, stepped inside and closed the door. "I wasn't expecting you."

She hadn't seen Brenda since the funeral. The woman's plump, middle-aged face still displayed the ravages of grief. Redness rimmed her eyes, and dark circles marked the skin beneath them. Morgan had always suspected Brenda's interest in her father had been more than professional. His secretary had unquestionably taken his death especially hard.

Brenda gave her another watery smile and rose from her desk. She looked ready to burst into tears. "I wanted to be here in case you had questions or needed help. You ought not tackle such a sad task alone."

"You shouldn't have—"

"Besides—" Brenda's nonchalance was obviously feigned "—I have work to catch up on."

Morgan repressed the grief Brenda's sympathy reactivated, and gave the older woman a hug. "I'll call if I need you. Thanks for being so thoughtful."

Brenda returned the hug, then grabbed a tissue. After a quick wipe of her eyes, she swung open the door to the inner office. "Nothing's been touched. I set a box on his desk, if you want it for carrying things."

Morgan entered her father's inner sanctum and closed the door. The woodsy aroma of his pipe tobacco permeated the room, and when she closed her eyes, she could almost believe her father stood next to her.

But he wasn't there, wouldn't ever be there again.

She opened her eyes and scanned the room, wondering where to begin. A framed picture of her with her father, displayed prominently on his desk, had been snapped last summer on a vacation to the Keys. Suntanned and windblown, they had laughed at the camera, blissfully unaware that less than a year later, he would be dead.

No time for memories now.

She choked back tears and began combing his

desk, glad for the presence of Brenda and the cleaning crews in the building. Between them and the watchful eye of plant security, a confrontation with Lashner's hirelings was unlikely, as Josh had promised.

She opened the top desk drawer and rummaged through its contents. Josh had instructed her to search for any documents or memos that might implicate Lashner, in case they had overestimated him and he had failed to remove incriminating evidence.

She scoured the desk, closets and the adjoining efficiency kitchen. After completing her inspection of the bottom drawer of the last file cabinet, she rose and stretched the cramps from her back and aching legs. Even though she hadn't really expected to find anything, she was disappointed she had uncovered nothing to tie Lashner to her father's death.

Brenda's empty box would not be needed. Her father had been a meticulous man who neatly compartmentalized his professional and private lives. Everything, except the framed photograph, related to his work. If he had kept this year's journal at the office, someone had already seized it.

"Finished already?" Brenda asked when Morgan entered the anteroom.

"There wasn't much. Dad must have kept personal things at home." Her glance fell on a small fire safe, half hidden by Brenda's L-shaped desk. "Unless something of his is in the safe."

Brenda shook her head. "I don't know why he bought that safe. He only kept one thing in it."

Morgan raised her brows. "Dad bought it, not the company?"

"I never could understand him spending his money," Brenda said, "because he used it for company business. He had a special file, one of those big accordion ones, that he placed in the safe every night."

Morgan kept her voice casual. "What was in it?"

"Oh, I never read it. But I watched him gather papers once and a bound book and shove them into it."

A bound book. The missing journal?

Morgan grew hot and cold simultaneously. "You're certain the papers weren't personal?"

"Your dad loved his work," the secretary said with another teary smile, "but not even Frank used chemical formulas to record his personal documents."

"Do you mind if I take a look at the folder, just in case?"

"*I* don't mind," Brenda said with a breezy wave of plump hands, "but you'll have to ask Mr. Lashner for it. He came in the day after your father...the day after the fire and requested all Frank's formulas. Said he didn't want Frank's untimely death to halt progress on an important project."

Morgan's hopes plummeted. The missing journal, which might have proved enough to hang Robert Lashner, had probably been destroyed by now.

She hadn't found anything to incriminate Lashner, but she suspected Brenda had other useful knowledge. The woman had worked for her father ever since he started at Chemco and knew more about Frank Winters than his own daughter did. Brenda had kept track of not only Frank's business appointments but his social calendar, too.

If the mysterious Josh really had been Frank's friend, Brenda would know.

Before Morgan could voice her question, she remembered the microphone between her breasts. No need to antagonize Josh with her inquiries. After springing the trap for Lashner tonight, she wouldn't need any corroborating information about the handsome private investigator. She would never see him again.

"Thanks, Brenda." She turned to leave.

"Wait. Where are you staying? Mr. Lashner said I should be sure to find out."

"With friends. Leave a message on Dad's machine if you need to reach me." Morgan slipped out and closed the door before Brenda could ask more.

The deserted stillness of the hallway roared in her ears. In her father's office with Brenda within shouting distance, Morgan had felt safe. Engrossed in her search, she had managed to forget briefly not only her hidden wire but the impending danger. Now the prospect of imminent peril swept over her with a vengeance, and she wondered if her courage was equal to the task ahead.

She was so wrought up that when the stairwell door clicked shut behind her, she jumped like water on a griddle and bounded down the stairs. Blood booming in her ears rendered her deaf to all other sounds. Had someone followed her, she couldn't have heard their approach.

When she reached the lobby, she ducked her head and whispered into the open neckline of her blouse.

"I hope you're close by. I'm in the lobby now and will be leaving the plant in a few minutes."

Images of Josh, his broad shoulders hunched over the receiver, his attractive face solemn as he monitored every sound, sustained her courage.

She exited the building and, restraining herself from running, marched purposely down the front walk. Her skin prickled ominously.

Someone, somewhere, was watching.

At her car, she dropped the keys and had to grope along the asphalt in the dark to find them. With wooden fingers, she unlocked the door, climbed inside and hit the control that activated the electric locks.

She caught her breath, along with the new-car scent of the interior, and doubted the luxurious, latest-model Lexus with its front and side air bags was really a rental car. Wherever Josh had acquired it, she was grateful, remembering the hit-and-run driver who had rammed her Volvo outside the cemetery. Only her car's side air bags and its indestructible chassis had saved her then.

The well-built car made her feel safer until she contemplated that the next attack might not come from a hit-and-run driver. In spite of Josh's earlier assurances she was safe inside the plant, her imagination galloped on fast-forward. Maybe a sniper, hidden on the roof of a building at the entrance to the industrial park, would take his best shot. Or perhaps they'd run her off the road and attempt to inject her with some lethal dose. Or maybe Lashner's men had already planted a bomb in her car.

Dear God, I wish I hadn't thought of that.

Reining in her fears, she rammed the key into the ignition with an unsteady hand and turned. When the quiet purr of the engine confirmed she hadn't been blown to bits, she backed out of the parking space and circled to the main entrance. The guard must have recognized her car, because he opened the steel gates at her approach.

She drove between them and picked up speed, eying the security guard in her rearview mirror as a reluctant sailor views the vanishing land.

"I'm through the gates and headed toward the highway," she said aloud, and wished her communication with Josh was two-way. She could have used some encouragement as she traveled the dark, lifeless streets of the industrial park.

Another check in the rearview mirror revealed a movement on the road. A vehicle without headlights had pulled in behind her. It couldn't have been Josh. His proximity would have alerted Lashner's men.

"Watson to Sherlock," she said with infinitely more calm than she felt, "the game is afoot. I'm being followed."

Another glance disclosed the dark silhouette of a second vehicle, too close to the first to be Josh. "Now my shadow has company."

When she reached the highway, a cluster of emergency vehicles blocked the road just south of the intersection. Their flashing lights strobed on two cars on the shoulder, hoods crumpled and windshields smashed from a head-on collision. Paramedics were lifting a man on a stretcher into an ambulance, and a policeman draped a sheet over a body beside the wrecked cars.

Her sympathy went out to the victims, and at the same time, she murmured a prayer of thanks that the road north of the intersection wasn't blocked. If she was forced to halt or choose a route unknown to Josh, she would have no defense against Lashner's men.

Josh had rented adjoining rooms in a motel ten miles up the unpopulated highway from the plant. If she reached the motel without interception, she would take one room, while Josh and Jim Dexter would wait in the other for Lashner's thugs to make their move. All she had to do now was concentrate on reaching the motel.

The trailing cars, headlights now blazing, turned onto the highway behind her, accelerated and closed the distance between them. Apparently, her pursuers were too impatient to wait until she reached her destination.

Morgan pressed the gas and checked the mirror to assure herself Josh and Dexter were following. The sight of the long, empty highway behind Lashner's vehicles made her stomach plunge like an elevator with a broken cable.

"I'm on the main highway with two cars in hot pursuit," she said. "Where are you?"

Speeding along the desolate road, she cast frantic glances in her mirror, hoping for Josh's appearance behind the convoy that chased her.

What was keeping him? Outside the limited range of the wire, he couldn't hear if she called for help.

And where was Jim Dexter?

A horrifying speculation burst into her consciousness. What if Josh's trap had been set, not for Robert

Lashner, but for her? Was treachery the secret she had glimpsed so often in Josh's eyes?

She forced the idea away as quickly as it came. Josh was Ben's friend and ally. Even if the investigator cared nothing for her, he wouldn't betray Ben.

Are you sure?

Panic was making her crazy. She had to focus on the instructions Josh had given her. For all she knew, he and Dexter could be rocketing behind her pursuers with their lights off.

Yeah, right.

She closed her mind to doubts. She needed Josh if she expected to survive.

"Josh." She called his name like a prayer.

She approached a curve, and the car behind her pulled alongside and nudged into her Lexus, forcing her right wheels onto the uneven shoulder.

Maintaining her speed and fighting the wheel for control, she risked a quick look at her assailant, but tinted windows in the late-model black van obscured both its driver and any passengers.

In a spurt of speed, the black van pulled ahead and the car behind her, a dark sedan, took the van's place alongside her. With their engines screaming in her ears, the two vehicles hemmed her in, closing off all escape.

Praying for Josh's arrival, she checked the rearview mirror.

Only darkness.

Ahead, the van slowed abruptly. At the same time, the sedan on her left cut its wheels, forcing her completely off the road. When she slammed on the brakes to avoid rear-ending the van, her car slid to a stop in a shallow drainage ditch.

The van halted in front of her, and the sedan formed a wedge between her and the road. In desperation, she threw the Lexus into reverse and gunned it, but the tires spun without traction in the deep muck of the ditch.

The driver of the sedan leaped out and sprinted toward her. Camouflage fatigues and a dark ski mask concealed everything but his ominous size. He rapped against her window with the barrel of a handgun the size of a small cannon.

"Get out, now," he yelled, "or I'll kill you where you sit."

WHEN BRENDA JERNIGAN told Morgan of Lashner's confiscation of Frank's mysterious file, Josh cursed and struck the dashboard with his fist. Having guessed right that Lashner got to Frank's papers ahead of Morgan gave him no satisfaction.

If she had found evidence to put Lashner behind bars, Josh would have gladly aborted their dangerous plan. He had no choice now but to carry out the scheme.

Quashing the desire to chuck everything and carry Morgan off to safety, he monitored her departure as she spoke first from the lobby, then outside the plant gates. Her humorous chatter and the bravado in her voice when she announced she was being tailed made him grin.

She was one spunky lady.

He started the Chevy, and his grin faded when the car choked and died. He turned the key again.

The engine revved, sputtered and quit.

With uneasy patience, Josh gripped the steering wheel. In contrast to the Chevy's dilapidated exterior, beneath its hood lay a powerful and finely tuned machine. His overzealous pressure on the gas must have flooded the engine. Every cell of his being screamed for haste as he endured the requisite delay before starting the car again.

He calmed himself with the reminder that Jim Dexter waited where the industrial park road entered the highway. As soon as Morgan's Lexus appeared, Dexter would fall in behind at a discreet distance.

"I'm on the main highway—" Morgan's escalating pitch implied panic "—with two cars in hot pursuit. Where are you?"

Restarting the car too hastily would only flood the engine again. He gritted his teeth and scrutinized the luminescent dial of his watch while the second hand crept forward with painful slowness.

"Josh?" Morgan's static-filled plea was almost indiscernible. She was leaving transmitting range.

When the hand of his watch had advanced to the allotted time, he twisted the ignition key and the powerful engine roared to life. He floored the gas, and the Chevy shot from its hiding place near the plant in a flurry of dust and the stench of burning rubber.

When Josh reached the highway, the first thing he saw was Jim Dexter's Bronco with its smashed front end and a sunburst of broken glass where Jim's head had hit the windshield. Someone had run off the road, straight into Jim's parked car.

His first inclination was to go to his friend's aid,

but Jim, if still alive, was being cared for by paramedics and policemen.

Morgan was alone.

Except for Lashner's goons, hot on her trail.

He rammed the gas as he turned north. The heavy car careened on its left wheels, threatened briefly to overturn and righted again. He accelerated, and the escalating whine of the engine tortured his ears. Ahead, as far as he could see, the highway lay dark and empty.

"Say something, Morgan," he begged between clenched teeth. "Let me know you're all right."

The receiver remained silent.

Chapter Eight

A double dose of guilt gnawed at Josh as he barreled down the highway. Jim Dexter was headed to the hospital—or worse—because Josh had hired him. The man had survived twenty-five years of active duty with the police department unscathed, only to be struck down by a careering car.

And if Josh didn't catch up with Morgan...

He damned himself with every curse he knew, then invented a few new ones. What a rock-headed idiot he'd been, risking Morgan. By now, with her backup missing, she would be terrified. If Lashner's men harmed her, he would never forgive himself.

He grimaced, struck by the painful irony that Ben would never forgive him, either.

Suddenly, above the massive engine's whine, static crackled from the receiver.

"Kill you..." the garbled transmission announced. Almost unintelligible, the harsh and menacing voice was male.

Lashner's thugs had Morgan.

Anguish skewered him with numbing despair. If he didn't reach her in time...

He refused to think the unthinkable. She couldn't be far away. On the open road, the transmitter range extended only a mile. Two at the most.

Her proximity reignited his flickering hope, and he increased his speed. The car surged forward and flew down the dark road. Pushing the Chevy to its limits, Josh skidded around a curve. In the distance, an emergency flare gleamed, and its sputtering flame cast an eerie red glow over tall pines beside the road.

Josh slowed as he approached, drew his gun from its holster and pulled the Chevy onto the shoulder.

Ahead, Morgan's Lexus rested in a ditch, the tires mired in mud, the driver's door ajar. Across the highway, two semitrucks were parked in tandem, half on, half off the asphalt, their presence marked with a warning flare.

Josh parked behind the Lexus, and the lead truck pulled away with a blast of its air horn. A second trucker remained in front of his rig and waved at the departing driver.

Josh holstered his gun, jumped from the car and rushed to Morgan's vehicle.

Empty.

A framed picture of Frank and his daughter stared at him accusingly from the passenger seat.

"Did you see the woman who was driving this Lexus?" he yelled to the trucker.

The driver, his lanky frame backlit by the headlights of his rig, jogged across the road. "Nope. Two other cars were here when me and my buddy drove up. We thought there'd been an accident and we stopped to help."

"An accident?"

"Yeah—" the trucker removed his cap and scratched his head "—'cause of the car in the ditch. Some feller was helping another big guy into a black van. Then the van and a blue Buick took off, headed north like bats outta hell. My buddy and me figured we'd stumbled onto some kinda drug deal and were lucky not to be shot."

"Was there a woman inside either vehicle?"

"Couldn't tell. Tinted windows." The trucker tugged his cap back on, started back to his truck, then turned. "You want me to call the highway patrol?"

With Morgan's life at stake, Josh needed all the help he could get. "Give them the description and direction of the cars and tell them you think a woman's been kidnapped."

The man ran back to his cab, started the motor and reached for his cell phone. "Handy things, these gadgets," he yelled across the road. "I just punch star-FHP to contact the Smokey Bears."

He pressed the keypad with a bony finger, lifted the phone to his ear and one-handedly maneuvered his rig onto the pavement and down the road.

Josh raced back to his car. He would drive north, and if he didn't overtake the vehicles the trucker had described, he'd go straight to Lashner.

If anyone had harmed Morgan, he'd kill Lashner with his bare hands.

Time was short, because Lashner's men wouldn't dare hold her long. The sooner they disposed of her and fled, the safer they would be.

He refused to believe he had already lost her, all she had been to him, all she would ever be.

When he reached the Chevy, a voice reverberated from the receiver.

"Josh? Where are you?"

Morgan!

He jerked open the door and slid behind the wheel. "Just feed me clues, and I'll find you," he begged, knowing she couldn't hear him.

"Josh—" her voice rang so loud and clear, she couldn't be far away "—if you find my car, don't leave. I'm nearby."

He bolted out of the car and yelled her name, begging her to speak again.

When the receiver remained silent, he returned to the Chevy and increased the receiver's volume, snatched a flashlight from the glove compartment and stumbled back to the Lexus.

"Morgan, can you hear me?" he shouted.

Only the wind soughing through the pine boughs, the screech of cicadas and the distant call of a chuck-will's-widow answered.

Playing the flashlight's beam over the ground, he searched the matted grass. The weeds, flattened by tires, displayed no hint of her footprints. Recalling how Morgan's slight weight had left no imprints in the wet beach sand, he held little hope of detecting her tracks, until he shone the light across the drainage ditch.

On the far side of the gully, a trail of black mud, stamped with the treads of small sneakers, disappeared into the words. Josh leaped the ditch and pursued the dwindling traces of muck across the pine needles carpeting the ground.

Every few yards, he called to her.

No answer.

He plowed deeper into the thick underbrush of the woods, until the vestiges of mud vanished completely. Fearing Lashner's men might return before he found her, Josh screamed her name into the stillness.

"Here—" the faint answer finally came "—over here."

Bulldozing his way through dense undergrowth that slowed his progress, he traveled in the direction of her voice. "Where are you?"

"Under a big oak—" her voice sounded stronger, closer "—in a field at the edge of the woods."

"I don't see a field," he called. "Run toward my voice."

Silence filled the forest.

"Morgan?"

"I can't" came her reply, weaker this time.

A legion of possibilities sprang into his mind. One of Lashner's men was with her, using her for bait. Or maybe she'd been shot before she escaped and was too injured to move. He pressed forward, oblivious to the branches thrashing his face as he ran.

Breaking into a clearing, he paused and turned off the flashlight. A broad moonlit meadow stretched ahead, empty except for a massive oak about a hundred feet away. The shadows of its spreading branches and heavy strands of Spanish moss hid whoever waited beneath.

An accessible target in the open field, he retreated into the pines. "Morgan, are you there?"

"I've twisted my ankle." Embarrassment rang in her voice.

Asking if she was alone was pointless. If Lasher's men were holding her, she wouldn't be allowed an honest reply. He tucked the flashlight into his belt, drew his gun and burst into the open, darting a zigzag course toward the tree. If a gunman awaited, Josh refused to provide him an easy shot.

In seconds, he covered the distance between the pines and the oak, and as his eyes adjusted to the darkness, he spied Morgan propped against the oak's thick trunk. He circled the tree, making certain she was alone, then scooped her into his arms.

"We have to get out of here fast," he said, "before they return."

Her arms clasped his neck, and her head nestled in the hollow of his throat. "I thought you had deserted me."

The disappointment in her voice increased his staggering load of guilt. "No time for talk now. I'll need all my breath to get us both back to the car."

With Morgan clutched against his heart, he loped back across the field toward the trees.

"How will we find our way back?" she asked.

"Pull the flashlight out of my belt and aim it ahead of us."

Morgan did as he asked, and for several minutes he searched up and down the treeline. When he spotted several broken branches, he lunged into the brush. Following the signs of his earlier passage, he labored back the way he'd come.

The heat of her body scorched his chest, blending with the ache of his old chest wound, but he welcomed the ferocious pain. The agony overrode the raging desire that had gripped him when he beheld

Morgan in the moonlight, her eyes wide with fear, her smooth cheeks wet with tears, the subtle scent of jasmine swirling in the night air.

He had wanted to claim her then and there beneath the oak, to love her to exhaustion to drive away the horror of the interminable minutes when he feared she was dead.

He had almost lost her once tonight. He wouldn't allow his seething hunger to jeopardize her again. Focusing on his pain, he forced one foot ahead of the other and struggled to breathe. If they could reach the car before the assassins returned, they'd be safe.

The whine of a speeding truck signaled the approaching highway, and Josh hovered at the edge of the woods until certain no one lurked near the cars.

Satisfied the coast was clear, he rallied the remnants of his strength, leaped the ditch and carried Morgan to the Chevy. He slid her onto the front seat.

"What about the Lexus?" she asked.

He sprinted to her vehicle. Pain expanded in his chest, slowing his movements and weighting his legs, as if he were slogging through mud. With labored breath, he retrieved the ignition keys and the framed photograph from the front seat and locked the car.

He struggled back to the Chevy, and bursts of red exploded behind his eyes. He stumbled to the passenger door.

"Twisted ankle or not," he said between clenched teeth, "you have to drive."

But before she could shift behind the wheel, he blacked out in her arms.

MORGAN CRADLED Josh's hand in hers.

Dust motes danced in the early morning sun slanting across his bed, the second sunrise since he had passed out on the front seat of the car. Scratches from his headlong rush through the woods crisscrossed his face, and a long-sleeved sweatshirt concealed his bandaged chest.

The assassin at the airport had injured Josh worse than she had guessed, and, according to the doctor, carrying her to safety again had reopened his injury.

The cool pressure of his fingers around hers signaled his awakening, and his eyes, clear and totally aware for the first time since his collapse, regarded her.

"Welcome back." Her joy flared like a rocket.

He furrowed his brow. "Where am I?"

"You're home. We're both safe now, thanks to you."

"Home?"

"At your cottage."

His puzzlement deepened. "How—"

"Harper carried you to bed. When you blacked out, I drove straight to Ben's."

His brown eyes widened with alarm, and he raised himself on his elbows, as if to climb out of bed.

"Don't worry." She nudged him back against the pillow, then smoothed the covers to hide her longing to touch him again. "Nobody followed. While Ben called the doctor, Harper drove us here and brought you inside."

"Where's the car?"

"Hidden in the garage. At night I've kept the curtains drawn and used only dim lights. From outside, the place still looks deserted."

Despite her protests, he shoved himself upright. "How long have I been lying here?"

Not long enough. "Since night before last."

He aligned his handsome mouth into a grim scowl. "That long?"

She nodded. "But only because I gave you sleeping pills with your antibiotics, at Dr. Hendrix's instructions."

"You drugged me?"

"He said it was either drugs or tie you to the bed." She raised her brows and tried to appear blameless. "He also says you're either more stubborn than an ox or else believe you're immortal. Where do you suppose he gets that idea?"

"Tom has a dictator complex," Josh grumbled.

Her innocent look faded. "You should be grateful he makes house calls. Ben insisted a hospital was out of the question, and no one but Dr. Tom be allowed here."

"Ben suffers from a dictator complex, too." A reluctant smile accompanied his griping. "How is Ben?"

"Dr. Hendrix demanded he stay in bed, so Ben relays messages to me through Harper."

"Shouldn't you be at home with your husband?"

She rationalized her guilt away. "He has Harper and Mrs. Denny to take care of him. You needed a nurse, so I volunteered."

"But your ankle?" His gaze flickered down her legs, fully exposed by her denim shorts.

Her pulse revved at the concern in his voice and the heat in his glance. "It's better. Dr. Hendrix wrapped it in an elastic bandage, and I've stayed off it as much as possible.''

Josh lay back and closed his eyes, as if drifting back to sleep. When he opened them again, remorse had turned them almost black. "And Jim Dexter?"

"He's in serious condition, but Tom's confident he'll recover without permanent injuries.''

"Did Lashner's men cause the accident?"

Lashner had them all suspicious of their own shadows. She, too, had feared Lashner's involvement until the doctor shared the details from the hospital report. "A drunk tried to pass a slow-moving car against approaching traffic. When he swerved to avoid an oncoming car, he hit Jim's, parked on the shoulder.''

"What about—"

"No more questions," she said firmly, noting the shadows beneath his eyes and the white edge to his lips. "Rest, and I'll fix your breakfast.''

His eyebrows soared. "You went shopping?''

"Of course not. Ben had Mrs. Denny bring us groceries. She even packed my clothes and sent them over. Ben's taken care of everything.''

"Not everything," he mumbled beneath his breath as she headed to the kitchen.

After feeding Josh the doctor's prescribed poached eggs, toast and tea, which she fortified with half a sleeping pill, she washed dishes in the sunny kitchen.

During her long bedside vigil, she'd had plenty of time for reflection. When Josh had kissed her on the beach, something sealed away far too long had broken free. His heat had kicked through her in a series of mind-numbing explosions, blasting the barricades of her desire. In that too-brief moment, she had sensed his matching response, but once he pulled away, his subsequent behavior, first flippant, then distant, had left her confused.

She pushed back her hair with the heel of a soapy hand and stared unseeing out the window above the sink. Had Josh been merely toying with her, or had he pulled away because she was Ben's wife?

Whatever the answer, something drew her with overpowering compulsion to the mysterious man asleep in the next room. Was it gratitude? Twice, not counting the diner incident, and at great personal risk, he had rescued her from disaster.

For which Ben was paying him handsomely.

Her heavy sigh scattered the soap bubbles in the sink. She shouldn't misinterpret Josh's dedication to his work as caring for her.

Rinsing the last of the dishes, she ranked her priorities. Number one was to assure that Lashner was caught. But in order to snare Lashner, she didn't *have* to work with Josh. Ben had a surplus of contacts and resources. He could easily find another investigator.

One who didn't make her spirit soar with delight or her blood run scalding when she saw him.

One who didn't hide secrets behind his too-fascinating eyes.

One who wouldn't break her heart when the job was done.

By the time she'd put away the last dish, her mind was made up. As soon as Josh was well enough to be left alone, she would return to Ben and demand he take Josh off the case.

WHEN JOSH AWAKENED for the second time that day, Morgan was sleeping in the big chair beside the bed. Her hair, the color of sunlit champagne, curled against the smoothness of pink-kissed cheeks. She frowned slightly, furrowing the skin between her brows and pursing delectable lips, as if dreaming bad dreams.

Bad dreams?

Nightmares, more likely, after what he'd put her through. And all for nothing. They were no closer to proving Lashner killed Frank than the day they started.

He shifted tentatively and braced for stabbing pain, but the wound in his chest pinched with only slight discomfort. He owed a debt of thanks to Tom Hendrix.

And especially to the woman in the chair beside him. Afternoon light filtered through the bedroom doorway behind her and shimmered like a halo around her silky hair.

She looked like an angel.

An angel who didn't deserve what Lashner had done to her, who didn't deserve what Josh had put her through. The greatest kindness he could show her was to catch her father's killer and get out of her life.

Forever.

His logic gored him with an agony more savage than any chest injury.

As if sensing his distress, she opened her eyes. Her slow, sweet smile only increased his torment.

"You're looking better," she said.

So are you. By the minute, he thought. "Sleep is a great healer. You drugged me again, didn't you?"

"Would you have stayed in bed if I hadn't?"

"I doubt it."

Her smile expanded. "I rest my case."

"While you're holding me prisoner, maybe you can tell me what happened on the highway the other night before I arrived."

Her smile faded, and she folded her slender legs beneath her and crossed her arms, as if safeguarding herself from the memory. "After the two cars forced the Lexus into the ditch, I was trapped."

His heart constricted at the residual terror mirrored in her eyes. "I'll never forgive myself for leaving you alone."

She threw him a puzzled look. "You had arranged for backup. It wasn't your fault Jim's car was hit."

"I'm the fool who flooded my car," he said with a scowl, "or I'd have been there when you needed me."

Her sky blue eyes harbored no blame. "Maybe things worked out for the best."

He snorted. "That's carrying optimism a bit far."

"Lashner had at least four men after me. Without Jim to help you, we both might have ended up dead."

"You escaped four men?" His admiration warred with delayed alarm.

She scrunched her face in a self-deprecating smile. "I can't credit skill or cunning. Just pure, unadulterated panic. At first, just one man jumped out of the dark sedan. When he threatened to kill me if I didn't go with him, I opened my car door."

Determination riveted through him. Before, his sole target had been Lashner. The hired thugs were only that scoundrel's means to an end. But one of them had frightened Morgan within an inch of her life, and that guy would pay, if Josh had to track him to the ends of the earth.

"I knew he was planning to kill me," she continued, "so I did what you told me. When he grabbed my arm, I blasted him with pepper spray."

"Did you get a good look at him?"

"His face was covered with a ski mask, so I aimed straight for his eyes and blinded him. Then the driver of the sedan came after me, but I sprayed him before he could draw his gun."

One small canister, almost an afterthought, had saved her. Josh collapsed against the pillows, overwhelmed with might-have-beens.

"And the other men?" he asked.

She hugged herself tighter but didn't stop shivering. "Everything seemed to happen in slow motion. With two men writhing on the ground, the pair in the van jumped out, guns drawn. When I took off running, I heard a truck approaching, downshifting. I plowed through the ditch into the woods, and I didn't stop until I twisted my ankle. In the dark, with my eyes watering from the pepper spray, I had tripped over a half-buried log."

"Those truckers were a godsend," he said. "When they stopped at what they thought was an accident, they scared your attackers away."

He wouldn't frighten her further by discussing what might have happened if the truckers *hadn't* arrived. Besides, she was a sharp lady. She already knew.

"I expected Lashner's men to follow," she said.

"I didn't know where you were, so I kept talking into the mike, hoping you'd hear and find me before they did."

Anger boiled over him in a red-hot wave, at himself for placing her in danger, at Robert Lashner for his greed and ruthlessness, at the assassins who would have killed her without hesitation if she hadn't run.

"Josh?" She hopped from her chair, leaned over him and pressed the smooth, cool skin of her wrist against his forehead. "You look feverish."

At her touch, his anger transformed to desire, an overpowering need to hold her, to feel the warmth of her flesh, the pulse of her heart, the sweetness of her breath.

Except for a quirk of fate, her precious life might have been snuffed out by an indifferent killer. He craved reassurance that she lived and breathed, in spite of what he'd put her through.

He reached out, twined his arms around her waist and pulled her onto the bed beside him.

Resisting, she braced her hands against his shoulders. "Josh, your wound—"

"To hell with it."

"I can't. I'm Ben's—"

"To hell with Ben." He clasped the back of her head and drew her closer until his lips touched hers. "I almost lost you."

"But you didn't." Her lips moved against his, and her resistance ebbed. "I'm perfectly okay."

Tugging her nearer, until she lay against him, he groaned with longing. "Morgan, you are *not* okay."

"What?" She struggled in his arms.

"You are perfection."

"Oh, Josh." She ceased resisting and surrendered to his kiss.

His mouth devoured her, tasted her sweetness, incited her response. She wrapped her arms around his neck and yielded to him, opening her mouth to his kiss. Low murmurs of desire issued from the back of her throat as he skimmed the soft curves of her shoulders, ran his hands beneath her shirt and cupped her firm breasts.

She arched beneath his touch.

With a smooth movement that caused only a small pain in his chest, he drew her on top of him until the length of their bodies joined. Her supple thighs pressed against the undeniable hardness of his arousal.

He broke from the kiss and cradled her face in his hands. Her blue eyes, glazed with passion, met his.

"Morgan, let me love you."

Chapter Nine

"You have to fire Josh." There, she'd said it. Morgan clasped her hands behind her to stop their shaking.

Ben's head snapped up at her words, but he said nothing.

Thankful his dark glasses absolved her from looking him in the eye, Morgan paced his enormous living room.

Hours ago she had fled Josh's cottage, horrified she had come within a heartbeat of succumbing to his tempting invitation. Her cheeks flushed with the memory, and she drowned desire with anger. Any man with that much energy no longer needed nursing care. If anything, he needed his brakes relined. Had her common sense not taken charge, where would she be now?

In his arms. In his bed.

She blocked the enticing picture from her mind.

When she had called Harper to come for her at the cottage, she intended to confront Ben as soon as she arrived at his home, but both the valet and Mrs.

Denny had insisted their employer not be disturbed until he awakened from his afternoon rest.

For three interminable hours, she had waited, stoking the flames of her anger and strengthening her resolve by cataloging Josh's faults.

"Fire Josh?" Ben flipped the toggle on his motorized chair and rolled toward her, cutting her off in the far corner of the room and ending her pacing. "You're not serious?"

She backed into an easy chair and sat, ankles crossed primly, hands folded in her lap. Earlier, as soon as she reached her room, she had stripped off the clothes that tortured her with Josh's scent and showered away the heat of his caresses.

"I'm deadly serious," she said.

"Why should I fire him? He's the best investigator I have." The gentle calmness of Ben's voice contrasted sharply with the harsh agitation in her own.

She numbered her accusations on her fingers. "First, he's accomplished nothing in all this time. He's found no evidence against Lashner."

Ben sat without moving. "Go on."

"His last scheme almost got me killed." Righteous indignation stiffened her spine.

"But he also rescued you. That's the second time he's saved your life." Ben adjusted his oxygen mask. "Doesn't that count for something?"

"I suppose." Antagonism wasn't producing the desired results, so she relaxed her posture and softened her voice. "He's also not well. He suffered a serious knife wound when he confronted Lashner's man at the airport. Dr. Hendrix said he should be resting, not working."

"I'm sure Josh will be touched by your concern." Even Ben's bandages couldn't conceal his wry smile.

"You're not going to tell him what I've said?" If he did, it wouldn't matter. She wanted Josh out of her life.

"You've given me three reasons. Anything else?"

I'm your wife. I care about you, and I'm falling in love with him, she screamed inside. *When I'm with him, I can't think straight, and my heart and body have wills of their own. I can't risk loving a man I know nothing about.*

She squelched her internal clamor. "No, that's all."

"You look flushed." Ben wheeled closer and rested his bandaged hand on hers. "Are you ill?"

"No," she lied, sick at heart, her pulse still galloping at the memory of Josh, stroking her face, her shoulders, her breasts, his body fused to hers.

Ben withdrew his hand, and she fidgeted beneath his silent scrutiny, intense even through the filter of his glasses.

"You would tell me," he asked, "if Josh has offended you in some way?"

"Offended?" She jerked her chin up, and her mouth gaped.

Did Ben know?

"Has Josh done something to upset you?" he asked.

She stared at the Aubusson rug, wishing it would open at her feet and swallow her whole. Ben had been thoughtful and more than kind.

He had trusted her.

And her uncontrollable response to Josh had betrayed that trust.

She regarded Ben too highly to lie to him, so she simply ignored his question. "Josh should be fired for the reasons I've given." She tried but failed to rekindle her former fury. "Otherwise, Lashner will never pay for murdering my father."

"Convicting Lashner is exactly why I must retain Josh," he said. "There is no one I trust more."

Trust Josh? A man with dark secrets lurking in his eyes, a man willing to make love to another man's wife? His *friend's* wife? Ben obviously didn't know Josh as well as she did.

She bit back an ironic reply. "Why do you trust him?"

Ben sat quietly, as if contemplating her question. His composed certitude, his refusal to be rattled by uncontrollable circumstances, and his extravagant regard for her welfare produced an island of serenity, even in the midst of the chaos that had begun with her father's murder.

She longed to claim that peacefulness as her own. Avoiding Josh and the warring emotions he generated would be a good start.

"I trust Josh," Ben said, "because I understand him. He and I are a great deal alike."

The absurdity of his statement stole her breath away. "You're not anything like—"

"Excuse me, Mr. Wells." Harper appeared at the door to the foyer and interrupted her chance for rebuttal. "Mr. Appel is at the gate and wishes to speak with you. He says the matter is most urgent."

Ben didn't hesitate. "Show him in."

Harper disappeared as quietly as he'd arrived.

"Shall I leave?" Disappointment rang in her voice as she contemplated the unexpected delay. After waiting so long, she had hoped Ben would settle the issue of Josh's employment quickly.

Ben shook his head. "Terrence Appel is a member of Chemco's board of directors. You'd better hear what he has to say."

Chemco's board was the least of her worries. "Will you fire Josh?"

"I'll have to think about it." He wheeled toward a group of chairs in the center of the room. "Come sit beside me and follow my lead."

Wondering how long Ben would take to decide Josh's fate, she exchanged her chair in the corner for one next to him. Moments later, Harper ushered an older gentleman into the room, then withdrew and closed the doors.

Although at least seventy, Terrence Appel moved with the vigor of a much younger man. His face, lined with age, was tanned and ruddy with seeming good health, and his clear blue eyes gave the impression of missing nothing. He crossed the room in three long strides to shake Ben's hand.

"Sorry to disturb you, my boy." Appel's booming voice matched the vitality of his appearance. "But strange things are happening I felt you should know."

"It's good of you to come." Ben nodded toward Morgan. "You've met Morgan Winters, Frank's daughter?"

"Of course. At the funeral." Appel approached and enveloped her hand in both of his. "I'm so sorry about your father, my dear. He was a first-rate chemist and a remarkable man. Chemco is much the poorer without him."

"Thank you." She said no more, ceding control of the conversation to Ben.

"How are you, Ben?" Appel's leathered forehead wrinkled in concern. "There've been so many blasted rumors—"

"As well as can be expected," Ben said. "Have a seat, Terrence, and tell me what brings you here."

Appel sat on the edge of his chair, his physical tension a stark contrast to the casualness of his canary yellow shirt and green-plaid golf slacks. "It's Rob Lashner. He's causing trouble."

Morgan stiffened at Lashner's name, but Ben appeared unperturbed.

"What's Rob done?" Ben asked.

"You know about the upcoming board meeting?" Appel asked.

Ben nodded.

"Rob came to see me this morning with some pretty harsh accusations. Said I should be aware of certain circumstances before the meeting." Appel cut his eyes toward Morgan, then back to Ben. "Perhaps we should discuss this in private."

Morgan started to rise, but Ben waved her back into her chair.

"Morgan," he said, "is a major shareholder in Chemco and will take Frank's place on the board. She should be aware of what's going on."

Appel scowled. "She'll never sit on the board if Rob has anything to say about it. He's filed a lawsuit to contest her appointment."

Fury exploded in Morgan and ate at the lining of her stomach. She'd harbored no doubts of Lashner's ruthlessness, but his infelicitous lawsuit, coming out of left field like a wild throw, stunned her.

Ben's bandages hid his reactions to Appel's announcement, and his voice remained calm. "Lawsuit? On what grounds?"

"Rob doesn't need grounds," Appel said. "He has friends on the bench who'll drag the suit out, delay hearings, grant continuances. Hell, I could be dead and buried before the suit ever comes to trial."

Ben turned to her. "Have Lashner's attorneys contacted you?"

Morgan shook her head.

Appel issued a gruff snort. "How can Lashner contact her when nobody knows where to find her? He's informed everybody else—me, Rhonda Covill, William Holton."

"Everyone on the board except me," Ben observed.

"He wouldn't dare come to you with the tales he's spreading," Appel said. "The man's up to no good. He seems more interested in his own glory and wealth than the interests of the company."

Morgan's interest in Appel quickened. With his blatant animosity toward Lashner, the old man might prove a valuable ally in keeping the dangerous gasoline substitute off the market.

"Those are serious charges." Ben's bandaged face and covered eyes revealed nothing of his reaction to Appel's words. "What's Rob been saying?"

"He's claiming you suffered head injuries in the explosion that have affected your sanity." Appel studied Ben as if seeking verification of Lashner's claim. "From what I can tell, your mind's as sound as ever."

"What's Rob's point?" Ben asked.

Morgan suppressed a smile. Ben knew full well what Lashner was up to. He merely wanted Appel's slant on his opponent's tactics.

"Rob contends you've made crazy claims about an instability in Frank's last discovery, that you blame the compound for the lab explosion and are totally irrational about keeping the formula off the market." Appel spread his hands wide. "Let's face it. The sale of a substitute for gasoline could make us all billionaires. I can't blame Rob for being antsy at the possibility of anybody discrediting the product."

Morgan scooted forward in her chair. Appel had to be convinced of the compound's danger. "Dad's formula—"

"Can be discussed at the board meeting," Ben interjected smoothly, "with everyone present."

Appel turned his shrewd attention to her. "Lashner said you would back up Ben's crazy claims. He implied you want your father's discovery and its profits all to yourself."

Morgan opened her mouth to protest but caught the brief shake of Ben's head and kept silent.

Ben activated the control on his chair and wheeled toward the foyer doors. "Terrence, I appreciate your telling me about Rob's lawsuit and other charges. Perhaps he and I should have a little chat before the board meeting. I tire easily these days, so if you'll excuse me..."

Appel shoved to his feet and walked to the doorway, where Harper appeared as if by magic to escort him out. When the double doors had closed behind his visitor, Ben turned back into the living room.

"What are you going to do about Lashner's lawsuit and his wild stories?" Morgan asked.

A ghost of a smile was visible through his bandages. "Exactly what he wants me to do."

"What's that?"

Ben's shoulders sagged with fatigue. "First I need some rest and time to think."

In light of his obvious weariness, she hated to burden him more, but no matter what Ben decided about Lashner, she couldn't face working with Josh again. "What will you do about firing Josh?"

He raised his head and gazed at her behind the opaque lenses of his glasses until she turned away from his scrutiny. "I'll tell you what I've decided tonight after dinner."

The wheelchair motor whirred softly, and when she turned around again, he was gone.

MORGAN ATE DINNER alone at the elongated dining table. Mrs. Denny, in her inimitably snooty fashion, had informed her that Mr. Wells would dine in his room and meet her on the terrace after eight.

Brooding over her inability to ferret out proof of Lashner's guilt or to resist Josh's appeal, Morgan picked at her beef bourguignonne and drank too much red wine. By the time Mrs. Denny had cleared the untouched dessert from the table, Morgan's head buzzed with frustration and slight intoxication. Hoping the brisk night air would clear her mind, she abandoned the dining room.

The grandfather clock in the foyer was striking eight as she entered the dimly lit living room. Harper stood by a door opened to the terrace.

"Mr. Wells is waiting for you on the lower level, madam. Please watch your step. His eyes are bothering him, so I've turned off the outside lights."

She crossed the terrace and moved out of the circle of illumination cast by the living room lamps. At the far side of the upper level, she paused to allow her eyes to adjust to the darkness. Starlight brightened the surface of the gulf, and in the distance, running lights of a fishing boat winked in the blackness.

Gradually she distinguished the encircling high wall that divided the lawn from the beach, the stairs to the lower terrace and Ben's dark form in his wheelchair, barely discernible beneath an arbor of dense bougainvillea.

Giddy from wine and the fear Ben might refuse her request to dismiss Josh, she trod carefully down the steps. When she reached within a few yards of him, she could still see nothing but his silhouette against the night.

A strange reluctance to confront her problems seized her. How much nicer simply to enjoy the starlight, the gentle night breeze and the heady fragrance of night-blooming jasmine in the air.

"Are you feeling better?" She took a seat in a wrought-iron patio chair a short distance from the arbor.

"More rested, at least." His wheezy voice floated eerily from beneath the darkness of the vines.

She suppressed a shudder. This was Ben, after all, her father's trusted friend. The husband she'd grown fond of. She had nothing to fear.

The semitropical night seduced her with its sounds and scents, and the tender caress of the breeze resurrected memories of Josh, his embrace, his lips on hers.

Ben spoke again, shattering her reveries. "Have you figured out what Lashner's up to?"

"Besides trying to kill us?" she answered in confusion.

"Killing us is his primary goal, of course. His lawsuit and rumor-mongering are only means to that end."

"I don't understand." She thrust thoughts of Josh into the back attic of her mind and slammed the door. She owed Ben, her husband and protector, her full attention. They could deal with Josh later.

"By filing suit to keep you off the board, and by going to Terrence Appel, Rhonda Covill and William Holton with tales of my mental instability," Ben explained, "Lashner is trying to force me into the open. Only with a personal visit to each individual on the board can I counter his accusations and garner the votes I need while your voting rights are in legal limbo."

"You don't have to go out in public. You could invite them here."

"By refusing to leave my home, I would appear weak. And such eccentric reclusiveness would reinforce his portrait of my dementia."

She wished she could see his face. Between Lashner's threats and Josh's attentions, her nerves were already overstrung. Talking to a shadow only added to her tension.

"The moment anyone speaks with you," she said, "they'll know Lashner is lying. You're one of the sanest men I've ever met."

"Sanity is a hard quality to judge, especially when doubt has already been planted in the observer's mind. But thanks for your vote of confidence."

She could hear the smile in his voice, and her jitters eased, until he spoke again.

"With his legal action and rumor campaign, Lashner has also thrown down the gauntlet to you."

She choked back a caustic laugh. "As if murdering my father wasn't challenge enough."

"So far, Lashner has been unsuccessful in locating you." Ben's distorted voice drifted from the shadows. "He's probably assumed we're in touch, that I'll divulge how he's slandered you."

"He's tried twice to have me killed." The words left a bitter taste on her tongue. "Surely he doesn't believe I'll do something foolish just because he's added legal briefs and name-calling to his attacks?"

"My guess," Ben said, "is that he's hoping you'll be compelled to defend your motives by confronting the board members with the truth."

She shivered in the warm night breeze as the implications of Ben's words hit home. "If either or both of us venture out in public to meet with these people, we become accessible targets for his hit men."

"His scheme is obvious. If he can't eliminate us before the board meeting, he will at least have thrown doubt on our credibility. And his lawsuit prevents you from voting. Lashner's betting the board won't take the word of a brain-injured invalid or a greedy daughter. Without your ballots to stop them, they'll vote with him to sell the formula.''

With nerves wound like a spring, she bounded to her feet and paced the flagstone terrace. ''We can't let that happen. If the compound is produced, hundreds of innocent people could die horrible deaths in the resulting explosions.''

''In the overall scheme of things, a few hundred deaths among millions of users would be merely a statistical hiccup.'' Irony edged Ben's voice. ''Sometimes it takes years to pull a faulty product off the market. Just ask Ralph Nader.''

A black depression washed over her. ''And the blame would be laid at my father's feet, while Lashner and his billions in profits will have conveniently disappeared. We can't let that happen.''

''I don't intend to.'' Ben's voice rang louder and stronger on the night air. ''I've sent the formula to three independent labs for testing. I hope we'll have their results in time for the board meeting.''

Gratitude merged with her affection for Ben. ''Thank you, for my father's sake.''

''The battle isn't won yet. I'm certain Lashner will present a few independent studies of his own to contradict ours. But if we can prove he killed your father to gain control of the formula, his proposal to sell it won't stand a chance of board approval.''

Morgan sank into her chair, and its cold, filigreed iron bit through her clothes. ''We're back to square one, then, without a scrap of evidence that Lashner is a murderer.''

"We have over a week before the board meeting, and I have a plan."

"You and Josh had a plan before, and look where it got us."

"I was wrong to place you in harm's way. This time *I* will be—how did you put it a few days ago?— the sacrificial lamb."

"But you can't," she said with alarm. "You're not well."

"Tom Hendrix says with a couple more days' rest, I'll be strong enough for what I have in mind."

Uneasiness replaced her alarm. "What *do* you have in mind?"

The chair's motor hummed as he rolled from beneath the arbor, but in the moonless night, he remained only a silhouette, barely visible against the backdrop of dark green leaves. "I've considered very carefully your request that I dismiss Josh."

Her heart suspended its beating and her lungs couldn't draw air. "And?"

"I'm going to fire him and send him away. You'll never have to deal with Josh again."

He had agreed to her demand, but his acquiescence gave her no pleasure. Instead, at his words, a yawning emptiness opened inside her.

"I'm your husband, your father's friend, and the CEO of Chemco. It's my responsibility to bring Lashner to justice for what he's done to you and to the company."

She gripped the iron arms of the chair.

"From now on," he continued, "we will appear in public together, call on the board members as a team. Maybe even confront Lashner himself."

His words barely registered. Her devastation at never seeing Josh again crushed her mind, tortured her body.

His chair whirred as he wheeled to the table beside her. "I think it's time you had a good look at the man you married."

His dark glasses clinked against the tabletop, and the oxygen mask dropped beside them. Light flared from a match as he lighted a citronella candle atop the table. In the resulting illumination, he turned, his face and hands free of bandages.

For the first time, she looked at her husband's face. Josh's deep brown eyes stared back at her.

Chapter Ten

Shock.

Disbelief.

Unmitigated fury.

Ben watched emotions dart like thunderheads across Morgan's face and, although he'd expected some repercussion to his deception, the magnitude of her anger staggered him.

"You!" She clenched her fists on her lap as if holding back from an attack, and her eyes blazed like blue fire in the candlelight. "How dare you!"

"You have every right to be furious—"

"Furious?" She spat the word at him. "Furious doesn't come close to how I feel." Wariness joined the anger in her eyes. "Where is Ben Wells?"

His heart lurched at the distress he'd caused her. He'd lied and pretended about almost everything— except loving her—and he wouldn't blame her if she never forgave him. The prospect terrified him. If she didn't, his life would never be the same.

"*I* am Ben Wells. And I'm also Josh. Benjamin Joshua Wells."

She jumped from her chair and backed away. "You could be the devil himself, for all I know."

"I have documentation in the house, papers and photographs, to prove my identity. Morgan, I swear to you, I will never lie to you again."

"You've got that right," she fired back. "I won't stick around to give you the chance."

She pivoted on her heel and would have run if he hadn't leaped from his chair and grabbed her hand. "Wait."

She jerked from his grasp.

"Please," he begged, "let me explain. Then, if you still want to leave, I won't stop you."

He held his breath as she hesitated. If she walked out now, he would lose her forever. Lashner's hired killers were waiting for her.

She stomped back and flung herself into a chair. "I'll listen. But I can't imagine any excuse to justify what you've done."

He exhaled in relief. "I didn't say I could vindicate my actions. I can only share my motives."

"Why did you trick me?" The pain in her voice stabbed him with fresh guilt.

"I admit, in retrospect, my plan appears absurd. But when you first arrived, I had to learn whether I could trust you. Having Josh, my alter ego, interrogate you seemed like a good idea at the time."

She lifted her face and unshed tears glistened in the candlelight. "You haven't trusted me enough to tell me until now?"

"No, you mustn't think that." Sensing the anger still seething beneath her tears, he restrained from wrapping his arms around her. "After that first night at the cottage, I was totally convinced I could rely on you."

"Why didn't you tell me then?" She glared, unforgiving.

"You were angry at Josh, and I wanted to convince you not to leave. If you had known Josh and I were one and the same, I would've had no chance of persuading you." He dragged a chair close, sat and leaned toward her, elbows on his thighs, hands clasped between his knees.

"But I left that night, in spite of your protests," she said in a softer tone.

"Yes, and too quickly for me to explain. When I rescued you at the airport, you knew me only as Josh, so I maintained the deception until I could bring you back here safely."

"You could have told me then." Her expression and voice hardened.

"I had intended to tell you the afternoon I returned from the hospital."

She pressed her fingers against her temples, as if her head hurt. "Why didn't you?"

He straightened and raked his fingers through his hair. "You confronted me immediately with your suspicions and distrust of Josh, because your father hadn't mentioned him in the journals. But you still trusted Ben. If I had confessed then, you wouldn't have had faith in Ben, either."

"Clearly with good reason."

He winced at her bitterness. "If I had confessed, you would have left again. I knew Lashner had a killer waiting, watching for you."

She stiffened. "You also knew you'd have no one to bait the trap for Lashner if I left."

He recoiled at the sting of her accusation, unable to refute it. If he lived to be a hundred, he would never forgive himself for the danger in which he'd placed her. "I underestimated Lashner. Had I foreseen how many men he has working for him, I would never have put you in such jeopardy."

He stared past her toward the gulf, where the running lights of a boat bobbed about two hundred yards off the beach, too close for good fishing. As a precaution, he leaned over and blew out the candle so that darkness protected them from prying eyes on the distant vessel.

"Why choose now to tell me?" she asked. "You could have pretended to fire Josh, and we could have gone on as before."

Because I love you.

But he couldn't confess that now. She wouldn't believe him. He settled for half the truth.

"From now on, I can't allow you to go out alone. And I must shed my bandages and wheelchair to look strong and well when we confront the board members. My appearing in public will draw Lashner into the open. Eventually he'll make a mistake, and when he does—"

From the corner of his eye, he saw a sphere of eerie green light materialize on the fishing boat and float above the deck like St. Elmo's fire. Then the strange glow abruptly disappeared, and a chrysanthemum of red flame blossomed in its place.

He lunged from his chair, grabbed Morgan and slammed her to the terrace beneath him as bullets whined overhead and spattered the house's brick facade.

"What happened?" Morgan attempted to rise.

He held her fast, lifting his head only far enough to signal Harper, who rushed indoors from the upper terrace. "Lie still. The shooter's on a boat off the beach."

"Let me up." She struggled against him. "It's pitch-dark. He can't see us."

The warm, soft curves of her body melded with his, and the sweet fragrance of soap and her singular scent filled his nostrils. Despite the present danger, heat cascaded through him, pooling in his groin.

"The shooter is using a starlight scope." He focused on the old pain in his chest and his freshly bruised elbows and knees to cool his desire. "The scope's green glow cast light on the sniper's face."

"I never heard of a starlight scope." She squirmed beneath him, and her movements taunted him with agonizing pleasure.

"It draws light from the stars to provide night vision. If we raise our heads above this balustrade, he'll blow us away."

"What do we do?" Her sudden stillness indicated she had finally grasped the gravity of their predicament.

"Harper's calling the police." To shield her from the cold surface of the terrace, he wrapped his arms around her, drew her closer and tucked her head beneath his chin. "We wait."

"For what?" she mumbled against his chest. "Daylight, so the gunman will have a clear shot?"

"The sniper can't chance hanging around. For all

he knows, the police are on the way." He caressed the silky softness of her hair and shuddered at how close he'd come to losing her.

A siren wailed on the distant highway and amplified as it approached the house. On the water, the boat's powerful engines surged to life. From the direction of the receding sound, Ben estimated the vessel had headed south, toward town.

Unwilling to risk a parting shot from the sniper, Ben refused to release Morgan, even when the sirens arrived and tires squealed to a halt at the front gate. A few minutes later, running feet sounded on the upper terrace and strong arms lifted him off her.

"You okay, Mr. Wells?" Harper's inscrutable mask had slipped, replaced by tight-faced concern.

A policewoman assisted Morgan to her feet.

"Everybody inside, fast," Ben ordered. "There's a sniper out there with a night-vision scope."

He herded them up the stairs to the terrace and into the living room, where Harper flipped a switch that closed the drapery electronically.

The policewoman's partner, a tall, rangy man, entered the room. "Another team is searching the grounds, and I've called the marine patrol. Now, will somebody please tell us what the hell's going on?"

Ben glanced at Morgan, curled white-lipped and shivering in the corner of the sofa. "Harper, bring us coffee, please. Officers, have a seat. It's going to be a long story."

FIGHTING EXHAUSTION, Morgan packed her suitcase. Whatever action she decided on, she couldn't stay here. She had sat for hours while Ben reported to the uniformed officers his suspicions against Lashner, starting with her father's dying words and ending with the sniper attack from the boat. Later, when Detective Paxton arrived, Ben repeated everything, but she paid scant attention to Ben's details or the detective's responses and had spoken only to answer questions directed at her.

Ben's treachery had preoccupied her. Her mind still boggled at the fact her gentle husband and the fascinating private investigator she'd fallen in love with were the same person. Ben had lulled her with kindness and consideration. As Josh, he'd attempted to make love to her, undoubtedly hoping to insure her continued help in catching Lashner.

What a fool she'd been not to see it.

But Ben hadn't been alone in his deception. He'd had Harper, Mrs. Denny and Dr. Hendrix as co-conspirators. Ben's frequent absences had failed to raise her suspicions, because his unavailability fit the pattern he'd established the first week she'd spent here, before she'd ever met Josh.

She'd been duped by an expert.

Ironically, Ben hadn't comprehended that her resolve to apprehend Frank Winters's killer sprang from her love for her father and her intention to stay alive, not from some romantic attachment to the admittedly handsome private investigator.

That doesn't mean you don't love Josh, her rebellious heart mocked.

"How can I love someone who's not real?" she muttered with a scowl.

She flung the last garment in the case and slammed the lid. After the police had left, she'd faced three choices: return to Memphis, go into hiding alone until Lashner was convicted or continue to work with Ben to bring her father's killer to justice.

Detective Paxton had promised to investigate Lashner, but Ben's wily partner would have covered his tracks well. Without solid evidence, the police couldn't charge Lashner. Even if they did detain him, his hired assassins had their orders. Going home with killers on her trail would be suicide.

Hiding on her own didn't offer much more security. Without Ben's financial resources, she would quickly exhaust her limited funds. As soon as she used her credit card, Lashner could trace her and his killers would close in. She'd been lucky to survive until now. She wouldn't push her luck by striking out alone.

Brushing her hair off her face with her fingers, she rolled her shoulders to ease her knotted muscles. Pain shot through her right shoulder where Ben had slammed her onto the terrace. She closed her eyes and tried to forget the pressure of his warm, hard body, the strength of his arms as he shielded her. According to the police forensics team, the bullet dug from the house's exterior wall was in a direct line from the boat through her chair on the terrace. If Ben hadn't knocked her down, she would have been seriously wounded. Or killed.

She owed her life to Ben. Again.

Finally she narrowed her options. She had no choice but to remain with Ben until Lashner and his assassins were behind bars, both for her own safety and the debt she owed her father.

But staying didn't mean she would trust Ben with

her heart. After his monumental deception, she couldn't be certain whether he actually cared for her or valued her only for her usefulness in nailing Lashner.

She twisted her mouth into an unhappy smile. Two could play at Ben's game. She would take advantage of his contacts and resources to avenge her father, keep the flawed formula off the market and stay alive in the process. After she'd accomplished those goals, she'd annul her marriage to Ben and walk away.

With a broken heart.

"Nobody dies from a broken heart," she grumbled without conviction, taking a last look around the room that had been her home for the past few weeks. Straightening her shoulders, she lifted her suitcase and opened the door. Ben would be waiting at the foot of the stairs.

BEN ROLLED OVER and turned off the alarm, illuminated by morning sunlight curling around the edges of the curtains beside his bed. He'd slept straight through since yesterday afternoon. Sweeping back the covers, he stood and stretched, amazingly rested after his marathon session with Detective Paxton the night before last.

He had needed sleep. His body was still healing, and with lives at stake, he couldn't afford errors caused by fatigue. One slip, and Lashner's killers would have him and Morgan in their sights.

Yesterday he and Morgan had given their pursuers the slip. Dressed in gardeners' coveralls and hats, they had escaped the mansion undetected in the landscaper's van. After shucking their disguises and taking a circuitous route with multiple cab changes, they had met Tom Hendrix in a crowded mall parking lot. The doctor had driven them to the secluded cottage on the bay, which would serve as their base of operations until Lashner was caught.

Or until they were discovered and forced to move again.

Tom had insisted Ben go straight to bed, and he had been too worn out to protest. During their flight from the house, Ben couldn't talk to Morgan without curious cab drivers or Tom overhearing. She'd had more than thirty-six hours now to contemplate his deceit and the reasons for it. He wasn't proud of tricking her and wouldn't blame her if she had decided never to forgive him.

However, the choice between keeping her safe and keeping her trust had never been a tough one. He'd deceive her again, if deception meant keeping her alive.

He pulled on jeans and a shirt, slid his feet into deck shoes and headed for the kitchen. The aroma of coffee brewing announced Morgan had preceded him.

When he stepped through the doorway, she stood at the sink, gazing out the window at the gulf. If she'd heard his approach, she gave no indication.

"Good morning," he said. "I hope you slept well."

"Well enough." Her equable tone gave no hint to her frame of mind.

When she turned and the violet smears beneath her eyes belied her claim, he swore inwardly at the pain his deceit had put her through, then added a second, stronger curse for Robert Lashner.

After he had poured a cup of coffee and sat at the table, she slid into the chair across from him and cradled a coffee mug in her hands. She studied the steaming liquid as if its surface held clues to her fortune and refused to look at him.

A long, uneasy silence stretched between them before she spoke. "Were you really injured trying to save my father, or was that part of the hoax, too?"

Her skepticism skewered him with fresh remorse. His charade as Josh had thrown everything he'd told her into question. No wonder she doubted him.

As Ben, he'd kept his hands bandaged. As Josh, he'd worn gloves or kept his fists in his pockets or otherwise concealed. Now he laid his hands palms down on the table in front of her. Pink scar tissue from multiple burns and the wounds he'd suffered from flying debris stood out against his tanned skin.

Her breath whistled through her teeth as she inhaled at the sight.

She might as well see it all. He pushed himself to his feet, yanked his shirt from his jeans and undid the buttons. "I promised I'd never lie to you again. You should know the whole truth. Neither my lungs nor my eyes were damaged by the fire. The oxygen mask and dark glasses were only to disguise my voice and cover my eyes."

He tugged off his shirt, and an unidentifiable emotion deepened the blue of her eyes to navy.

"When I found your father in the burning lab, he warned that Lashner had planted a second explosive. I hoisted Frank on my back in a fireman's carry and covered him and my head with a flame-retardant blanket to protect us from the fire.''

She pressed her fingers to her lips but said nothing.

He skirted the table and stood beside her. ''When the second explosion hit, the blanket shielded your father and my head and face. The lab counters screened my legs, but my hands and chest caught the brunt of the blast.''

She gazed at the scar tissue covering his chest and pointed to the bandaged wound near his collarbone. ''Is that where the man at the airport stabbed you?''

He shook his head. ''When I carried you across the parking lot that night, the sutures gave way in a wound caused by a shard of flying glass in the lab explosion. I had to return to the hospital to have it restitched.''

''So you really were in the hospital?''

''Except for sneaking out, against Tom's orders, to accompany you to Frank's condo.''

She reached out and touched his puckered flesh with cool, gentle fingers. ''I'm so sorry.''

He covered her hand with his. ''The explosion wasn't your fault.''

''But I put you through so much exertion when you should have been recuperating. I should have listened to you instead of trying to run home.''

''You mustn't blame yourself.'' He tightened his grip on her fingers and tugged her from the chair. ''You'd just been asked to do some pretty scary things. Your reaction was understandable.''

She lifted her face, luminous with regret. Wrapping his arms around her, he drew her against his injured chest and lowered his head to claim the delicious pressure of her lips. He groaned with pleasure when she reached up and threaded her fingers through his hair, and the movement forced her closer, until the tautness of her nipples scorched his bare skin through the thin fabric of her blouse. Enclosing her tighter in the hot, tense circle of his arms, he deepened the kiss with a gentle flick of his tongue.

He wanted their embrace to go on forever. How could he live without this woman in his arms? Without her touch, her smile, the sweetness of her breath mingled with his? Without joining his body with hers?

As if sensing the direction of his thoughts, she withdrew, flustered, and slipped into her chair. An attractive blush colored her face. "So what do we do now?"

Love each other senseless, his heart answered.

But Lashner and his killers were still stalking them, and Ben's first priority would always be to keep Morgan safe. He clamped a lid on his desire, circled back to his chair and shrugged into his shirt. "We begin gathering support from the board members before the meeting. We'll need every vote, in case we can't put Lashner behind bars before the meeting."

"Isn't going out risky?" The breathlessness in her voice, like the glint in her eyes and the rosy glow of her cheeks, could have been fear or an after-effect from their kiss.

He forced himself to concentrate on business. "Lashner probably has someone watching Rhonda's house, hoping we'll show up, so we won't go there."

Her expression reflected conflicting emotions, as if

she, too, battled desire. His hopes leaped at the prospect that she might love him, even after his trickery.

Her face settled into sober lines. "Where are we going?"

"Do you play tennis?" he asked, and laughed at her expression of shocked surprise.

AFTER CHANGING into white shorts, a powder blue knit shirt and sneakers, Morgan joined Ben in the old Chevy for a ride to a quiet residential street several miles away. From there, they walked a few blocks to a grocery store thronged with early shoppers and caught a cab to the Gulfside Country Club.

Earlier, her anger at Ben had melted away at the sight of his hands and chest, scarred by his efforts to save her father, and she had allowed emotions to override her common sense. Ben *had* tricked her, after all. She couldn't give her heart to a man she couldn't trust.

Not even when her head argued his good qualities and her body craved him the way an alcoholic lusts for drink.

Sitting beside her now in the back of the cab, his long, bare legs stretched before him, he looked tanned and fit. Except for the scars on his hands, no one could tell the handsome executive in tennis whites had ever suffered an injury.

They reached the country club after a long drive up a private, palm-lined road that bisected one of three golf courses. The cab dropped them near the tennis complex, and Ben, outwardly relaxed, gestured toward the pro shop's second floor.

"There's a spectators' balcony up there," he said, "with a beverage bar."

They strode quickly along the narrow lane beside the rows of courts. Only the plunk of tennis balls against racket strings and an occasional call of score broke the morning stillness. Morgan preceded Ben up the pro shop's exterior stairs to the second floor, enclosed on three sides, its fourth open to a sweeping view of the courts. A quartet of ceiling fans circulated air above several small tables, and a snack bar occupied the back wall.

Morgan waited for Ben to select an empty table. He hesitated only briefly before leading her across the room to a table by the railing, occupied by a short, muscular woman with blunt-cut gray hair. She wore a tailored tennis dress with lace-trimmed panties peeking from beneath her abbreviated skirt, and her craggy face lit up like Christmas when she spotted Ben.

So this was Rhonda Covill, the only female member of the board. Morgan searched the older woman's face, but couldn't decide if Rhonda's pleasure at seeing Ben was genuine or feigned.

"Bless my tired old bones." Rhonda grasped Ben's hand and shook it with the vigor of a man. "I heard you were ready to curl up your toes and die."

Ben grinned. "As Mark Twain once said, rumors of my death have been highly exaggerated."

"And you're Frank's daughter." Rhonda greeted her with a handshake. "Such a waste. He was a damned good chemist."

Morgan winced at Rhonda's tight grip. "And a wonderful father."

"That, too, I'm sure. What are you folks drinking? I'll buy." Rhonda crooked a finger at the young woman behind the snack bar.

"Mineral water," Morgan said. Rhonda's too-hearty manner could be her usual demeanor or an effort to conceal her true feelings. Either way, the woman made her nervous.

Ben ordered mineral water, too, and they sat at Rhonda's table. The waitress returned immediately with their order, and Rhonda waited until the server left before speaking.

"What's going on, Ben? First that awful fire and Frank's death, and now Rob Lashner running around filing lawsuits and telling people you have a screw loose. And that you—" she glanced at Morgan accusingly "—are trying to cheat Chemco out of billions."

Ben sipped his water, then set down his glass. "Three attempts have been made on Morgan's life. Rob must want those billions pretty bad."

Rhonda's jaw dropped, and she glanced from Ben to Morgan. "Are you saying Rob tried to kill—"

"No doubt about it," Ben said.

"And you have proof?"

Morgan shook her head. "The police are working on it."

Rhonda's gaze met hers briefly, then slid away. "Ye gods, what's this world coming to?"

Ben leaned toward Rhonda and placed his hand over the older woman's. "Rob's been to see you?"

Rhonda nodded. "Gave me this cock-and-bull story about your brains being scrambled by your injuries from the fire. Said the board needs to keep you from doing something crazy, like destroying Frank's formula for a gasoline substitute."

"Dad's formula is flawed," Morgan said. "He feared people would be killed if the product goes on sale."

Rhonda assessed her with shrewd gray eyes. "That's what Rob said you'd claim."

"What else did Rob say?" Ben asked.

Rhonda's expression seemed pained. "That you wouldn't live until the board meeting. Your injuries were too severe. And with you dead, Morgan would return home, once her chief supporter was gone."

"I'm more than Morgan's chief supporter," Ben said with a warmth that made Morgan's cheeks burn. "I'm her husband."

Words failed the loquacious Rhonda, who glanced from Morgan to Ben in stunned silence.

"Rob Lashner—" Ben's voice was edged with steel "—is so blind with greed, he doesn't care how many people might die from Frank's unstable formula. With his dying words, Frank told me Rob had threatened him not to reveal the flaw, then set the fire that killed him."

"You can't be serious?" Rhonda's gray brows rose. "I know Rob's always been a go-for-the-jugular businessman, but a murderer? I don't believe it."

"Believe it," Morgan said. "Neither my father nor Ben is a liar."

At least her father wasn't. She recalled Ben's lies about Josh.

"I intend to have enough proof," Ben said, "by the time the board meets next week, to send Rob to jail for the rest of his life. All I ask is that you keep an open mind."

"Of course," Rhonda answered.

Too quickly, Morgan thought. Her instincts screamed not to trust the woman, and she worried that Ben had revealed too much. She wanted to leave before he said more. "We'd better go."

Ben rose, tugged his wallet from the back pocket of his tennis shorts and extracted a card. "If you hear anything, give me a call at home."

"I'm not sure I trust her." Morgan skipped down the exterior steps beside Ben. "She didn't tell us anything new."

"No, but we've accomplished our mission."

"Instilling reasonable doubt?"

"Exactly. Unless Rhonda is in league with Lashner—"

"You think she might be?"

He shrugged. "I'm the one who has trouble trusting people, remember?"

"So Josh told me."

He had the good grace to look chagrined. "Anyway, our visit with Rhonda calls Rob's credibility into question, unless I really do act brain damaged."

She paused at the foot of the stairs, tipped her head and considered him somberly. "I don't know how to break this to you, but—"

"Why, Morgan Winters Wells—" he broke into a smile "—you're teasing me."

The warmth in his expression eased her icy fears. If only she could be convinced he cared for her, that he wasn't simply using her to trap Lashner. Her head ached, as if it had been batted back and forth like one of the tennis balls she heard pinging on the nearest court. She had never doubted Ben's motives until he'd revealed how he'd tricked her.

Now, would she ever trust him again?

He draped his forearms across her shoulders, clasped his hands behind her neck and regarded her with a fondness that made the gold flecks in his eyes shimmer. "What about you, Miz Greedy Guts? Do you come by your rumored stinginess naturally, or do you have to work at it?"

"I do penny-pinching exercises every day," she answered with a straight face.

He tugged her closer, until her body fitted snugly against his. "I'm not usually a greedy man, but I want you all to myself."

She couldn't resist needling him. "You'd better talk to Josh about that."

Desire flared in his eyes. He lowered his lips, but the reference to his deceit cooled her longing, and she turned her head away.

"You asked me to remind you," she said, "to call Detective Paxton."

After a long studying look, he nodded and dropped his arms from her shoulders. "It's times like this I wish I didn't have to worry about Lashner monitoring my cell phone calls. There's a pay phone in the locker room. Wait here. I'll be right back."

He disappeared into a dark hallway behind the pro shop, and Morgan leaned against the rough cypress wall to wait, hidden from everyone except those passing on the adjacent walkway. She tipped back her head and closed her eyes. Without protest, she would gladly give a whole week's pay for just one good night's sleep.

Voices from the tennis courts, the whirring of distant golf carts, even the clanking of a soft drink machine in the hallway behind her faded. She dozed, oblivious to her surroundings.

"Why, Miss Winters," a cultured voice exclaimed. "What a pleasant surprise. I've been searching for you everywhere for weeks."

Her eyes flew open, and she looked directly into the face of her worst nightmare.

Just a few feet away, a tall, thin man with graying hair had halted on the walk. He approached and cornered her in the hallway. "How good to see you again, my dear."

Robert Lashner had found her.

Chapter Eleven

"Thanks, detective, I'll keep in touch." Ben hung up the receiver.

Unwilling to leave Morgan alone a second longer, he rushed out of the locker room and jolted to a standstill when he spotted Lashner.

Glancing quickly around the grounds, he detected no one who looked like Lashner's henchmen. But not recognizing them didn't mean they weren't out there. Thankful he had called for a cab before he'd phoned Paxton, he forced his tensed muscles to relax and sauntered toward Morgan and Lashner.

"What are you doing here, Rob?"

Lashner, who hadn't heard him approach, wheeled around. His chiseled features broke into a welcoming smile, reminding Ben of a fox in a henhouse.

"Ben," he said in a booming voice, "it's great to see you out and about. I've been worried about you, my boy."

Ben clenched his fists and held his temper. For two cents, he'd have gladly wiped the irritating smirk off Lashner's conniving face.

Morgan relayed Ben a look of relief. "Mr. Lashner

says he's been trying to contact me. I guess I should check Dad's answering machine more often.''

If coming face-to-face with her father's killer had rattled her, it didn't show, he thought, admiring her cool, collected poise.

He rammed his fists in his pockets, ignoring Lashner's outstretched hand. ''What brings you here? Not tennis or golf in that suit.''

Lashner dropped his hand to his side, but his smooth facade didn't crack. ''I'm early for a Chamber of Commerce luncheon at the main clubhouse, so I popped over to see Rhonda. She plays tennis every morning.''

''Really?'' Ben acted surprised, while suspicions raised the hackles on his neck. He wondered if Rhonda had called Lashner and told him Ben and Morgan were at the club. Rob's showing up was either intentional or a crazy coincidence. ''Give her my regards. Now, if you'll excuse us, we have a car waiting.''

''Of course.'' Lashner nodded to Morgan and turned away, then halted and approached them again. ''Do you know why a police detective visited me yesterday?''

Suppressing a satisfied grin, Ben shrugged. ''I've been cooped up at home, remember? You're not in some kind of trouble, are you?''

Lashner's suave mask slipped. Malice glittered in his eyes, and his words struck cold and hard, like bullets. ''No, *I'm* not the one in trouble.''

''Happy to hear it,'' Ben replied with fake enthusiasm, and placed his hand beneath Morgan's elbow. ''Sorry, but we have to run.''

Stepping past Lashner, he guided Morgan out of the hallway and around the pro shop to the parking lot. Forcing an unhurried pace, he felt the older man's stare boring between his shoulder blades. If the hired guns were around, they could grab Morgan and him at any moment, although an abduction in the club's parking lot, visible to tennis players, golfers and Chamber members arriving for lunch wouldn't be a smart move.

And Lashner was no dummy.

Nonetheless, when Ben found the cab waiting, relief blew through him like a fresh breeze. He opened the door for Morgan, then climbed in beside her.

"Take us to the nearest shopping center," he instructed the driver.

Morgan, her face pinched and pallid, sighed with relief. "Seeing you step out of the locker room was like a last-minute reprieve."

Ben jerked his head toward the cabbie in a silent warning to watch her words. "What did our friend say before I arrived?"

"Just that he's been trying to reach me. I restrained myself from mentioning the deadly shape his latest 'messages' had taken." Anger over the sniper who had almost killed her revived her color.

He reached for her hand, happy when she didn't pull away, and they rode in silence. Every few minutes, he checked the rear window. No cars appeared to be tailing them, but Lashner had enough money to hire the best, and a pro wouldn't allow them to spot him.

"Did you make your call?" Morgan asked.

"I'll tell you about it later." Ben scanned the landscape as the cab turned into the shopping center. "Driver, drop us in front of the department store."

When the cab stopped, Ben exited, gave Morgan a hand as she climbed out, and paid the driver.

"Where to now?" she asked as the taxi pulled away.

"Shopping."

"For what?"

"Another taxi. Lashner had a good look at this one. It'll be easy to trace." Taking her arm, Ben strode through the double doors of the store and paused at the first counter with an available clerk. "Is there a pay phone in the store?"

The cosmetics clerk batted her heavily mascaraed eyelashes and pointed toward the rear of the store. "Next to the rest rooms."

He started down the aisle with Morgan in step beside him. "I reached Paxton. He questioned Lashner yesterday, but Rob was at home, with twelve dinner guests as witnesses, when the sniper fired on us."

"I'm not surprised. He's too clever not to have an alibi. Did the police find the boat?"

"They checked every marina between here and the mouth of Tampa Bay, but they couldn't identify the sniper's vessel. I doubt it docked at a marina, anyway. Thousands of private slips line the coast. That boat could be hidden anywhere by now."

They entered the rear hallway and found the phone kiosk. He dug into his pocket for change.

Morgan, her forehead furrowed with worry, grasped his arm. "Paxton wasn't fooled by Lashner's alibi, was he?"

Overwhelmed by a desire to shield her from any

anxiety, he ran his finger down the soft curve of her cheek. "That's the good news. Paxton's put a round-the-clock tail on my esteemed partner."

"Good. Now Lashner's getting a taste of his own medicine."

The mixture of sweetness and sarcasm on her face enticed him, but her safety took precedence over his longing. He dropped a quarter in the slot, dialed a cab company and gave directions to a spot blocks away, a place Lashner would have a hard time connecting to them if he checked the taxi company logs.

When Ben hung up, Morgan headed back into the store.

He grabbed her arm. "Not that way."

Turning to the rear of the hallway, he opened a door marked Employees Only. In the stockroom, a middle-aged man was stacking boxes of dinnerware.

"Hey," he said with a bad-tempered growl, "you can't come in here."

Unperturbed, Ben ambled toward him. "Is there a back way out?"

"Yeah, but ain't nobody supposed to use it but employees. You'll have to leave the way you came."

Ben returned to the door they'd entered, opened it a tiny crack and peered out. His viewpoint offered an unobstructed vista of the front of the store. Entering the front doors behind a woman with a baby stroller was the thug who had attempted to kidnap Morgan at the airport. Two big guys in ill-fitting suits followed close behind. The poor cut of their clothes failed to conceal the bulge of shoulder holsters beneath their jackets. Lashner's assassins had caught up fast.

Ben drew back, shut the door and tried to purge the panic from his expression.

"What is it?" Morgan asked.

"Our friend from the airport and his pals," he whispered, "but don't worry."

He reached for his wallet, pulled out a fifty dollar bill and approached the stock man. "Hey, buddy, can you help a guy out? I'm really in a pinch."

He flashed the fifty, then leaned over and whispered in the man's ear.

The older man's ruddy face broke into a grin. He palmed the bill and shoved it in his pocket. "Right this way, folks."

They followed the stock man down an aisle between shelves piled high with inventory and through a curtained alcove into a dark hallway.

The man indicated an exit sign glowing red at the hall's end. "That door opens out back, behind the Dumpster."

Knowing Lashner's assassins were breathing down their necks, Ben didn't wait to thank their guide. He rushed Morgan straight to the door and out into the glaring sunlight. Surveying the area swiftly, he pointed to an almost imperceptible break in the head-high hedge lining the back of the shopping center lot. "That way."

Morgan sprinted to the hedge and slipped easily between the ligustrum branches into the backyard of a small ranch-style house. Ben followed, cursing silently at the valuable seconds wasted freeing his shirt that snagged on a branch.

He caught up with Morgan and headed up the driveway. "I hope you're up to a jog."

"Good thing we're both wearing sneakers." She followed his lead without question or complaint, as if they'd worked as a team their whole lives. He found her intriguing in ways he couldn't begin to define. If they came through this alive, he looked forward to identifying what made her so appealing.

But now wasn't the time to contemplate her allure. He glanced quickly over his shoulder. Their pursuers were not in sight, but the men could appear any minute. He had to widen the distance.

He and Morgan pounded up the drive and reached the curb of a deserted residential street. Together they darted across the road to the drive of the opposite house, through the open carport to the rear and straight into the adjoining backyard. They sprinted to the next street, turned right at the curb and jogged down the shaded avenue.

He had to be losing his mind. The troublesome wound in his chest ached, he labored to breathe, and they had three hired killers on their heels, but in spite of all that, he felt lighter and happier than he had in weeks.

Morgan, her lips softly parted, her skin glowing like porcelain beneath a thin sheen of perspiration, her glorious golden hair gleaming in the dappled light, inspired his irrational well-being. When she glanced at him, her sky blue eyes shimmered with acceptance, and the sweet tilt of her lips made unspoken promises.

Okay, so he was crazy, but he felt terrific. His burden of past deceptions and lies had lifted. She had learned the truth, and she didn't hate him for it.

He laughed aloud.

"What's so funny?" she asked without breaking stride.

She'd think him nuts if he confessed how happy he was. "I was thinking about the man in the stockroom and how quickly fifty dollars changed his mind about helping us."

She lifted one brow. "It took more than fifty dollars. What did you whisper to him?"

"You don't want to know." Alert for signs of pursuit, he glanced at the still-empty street behind him and kept his pace.

"No more secrets," she pleaded, "please."

He threw her a somber look. "I told him a private detective had just come in the front door, looking for us."

Her eyes widened with astonishment. "You told him we were criminals?"

"Not exactly. I told him my wife had hired the private eye."

"But I'm your wife!"

Joy shot through him at the fierceness of her declaration. "That's not what I told him."

Her blue eyes narrowed. "Who *did* you say I was?"

He tried to look gloomy. "A fallen woman who, if my wife learns about you, will break up my happy home."

Her jaw dropped. "A home-wrecker, am I?"

"With no morals," he deadpanned. "And greedy, too."

Before she could react, shouts of angry male voices and pounding feet pierced the lazy silence of the neighborhood. Lashner's thugs burst into the open a block behind them. Ben increased his speed and raced down the street with Morgan beside him. At the next intersection, he veered left and halted beside a cab parked at the curb, exactly where he'd told the driver to meet them.

"Hurry," he said.

Morgan dove into the car and collapsed on the seat. Ben scrambled in and gave the driver directions to where they'd parked the Chevy earlier.

Gasping for breath, she jabbed him with her elbow. "Called me a fallen woman, did you? Don't think you can ruin my reputation and get away with it. I'll have my revenge."

He checked the rear window. The cab had pulled away before Lashner's thugs had reached the corner.

He relaxed against the seat, smiled with satisfaction and reached for her hand. "So you plan to get even, do you? I look forward to it."

MORGAN EYED the dilapidated bar on the riverbank with skepticism. "You're certain this is the place?"

Ben nodded. "William Holton's best-kept secret. He hides here once a month until the members of his wife's bridge club have left his house."

Conversation kept her reactions under control. After their escape from Lashner's assassins, they'd returned to the cottage to shower and change clothes. The intimacy of that setting had increased the tension between them, tightening the bonds of their attraction.

That morning, when Ben had revealed the scars from his injuries, her anger over his deception had disappeared. How could she remain hostile when the man had suffered so much to help her father? The extent of his charade still irritated her, but his motives, at least, had been honorable.

This afternoon, after their run, when he had emerged from the bathroom smelling of soap, with a towel draped around his narrow hips and his hair slick with water, desire tinged with something deeper washed over her.

She had rushed past him into the bathroom and let her shower run cold. She could forgive, but she couldn't risk loving. If he had pulled such a whopping deception before, how could she judge whether he cared for her now?

Oh, he wanted her safe, all right. She was sure of that. But whether because he cared for her or simply needed her help remained to be seen.

Ben drove into a parking place behind a custom van that hid their car from the road. Dressed in pleated slacks that emphasized his flat stomach and a forest green madras shirt that turned the flecks in his eyes emerald, he looked more handsome than ever. He grasped her chin and pulled her toward him, skimming her lips with a butterfly kiss that left her aching for more.

Shock waves rocked her body at his caress. Wishing for another cold shower to purge her mutinous longings, she drew back. "We'd better hurry."

The warmth in his eyes indicated he'd misinterpreted her haste. "You're right. Let's get this interview over with."

While he circled to open her door, she fought the emotion that buckled her knees. Catching her father's killer and stopping the sale of the formula were paramount. She had to ignore the promise in Ben's eyes that startled her even more than his kisses.

"Do you think we'll learn anything new from Holton?" Thankful her voice relayed none of her inner turmoil, she accompanied Ben to the door of the bar.

"We won't know until we ask."

Stepping from the bright sunlight into dimness, she beheld a room that contrasted with its run-down exterior. The polished oak bar, decorated with mounted sailfish and seashells tucked in draped fishnets, ran down the right side of the narrow but spotless space. Across from the bar, booths and wide windows, overlooking a tranquil river, filled the other wall.

A few customers occupied bar stools, and in the far booth, a man was huddled with his back to them, nursing a tall drink. Ben led the way and slid onto the bench across from the him. Morgan scooted beside Ben.

William Holton glanced up, his mouth dropped open and a wide grin split his face. He pushed his drink aside and reached across the table to pump Ben's hand. "I thought you were a goner. You're the best news I've had in a month."

A display of such genuine affection would be hard to fake, especially at short notice. When Ben introduced her and she received the same response, Morgan warmed to the short, rotund board member with the balding head and beaming smile.

Holton's smile disappeared when he spoke of her father. "Frank and I had lunch together the day he died. 'Billy,' he told me, 'I enjoy my work, but the best days of my life are the ones I spend with my daughter.' Your father loved you very much, young lady.''

The gentle man with kind eyes had given her a priceless gift. "Thank you."

He nodded. "Now, Ben, what brings you here? Just passing through, like the time you first discovered my hidey-hole, or business?"

"Business." Ben's expression turned grim. "I understand Rob Lashner's talked with you."

Holton's mouth puckered, and his eyes squinted behind his wire-rimmed glasses, as if he'd tasted something sour. "Lashner's a damned liar. If you're crazy, I'm Mel Gibson. And as for Morgan being greedy, a man like Frank couldn't raise a greedy daughter."

Morgan leaned toward him. "Did Lashner tell you anything else?"

Holton jutted his receding chin in the air and closed his eyes as if remembering. Morgan held her breath, hoping he'd give them information to use against her father's killer.

The older man opened his eyes and shook his head. "No, just those slanderous accusations against you and Ben."

Her shoulders drooped with her spirits. Their search had hit a dead end.

"But Frank said something," Holton added.

"What?" she and Ben exclaimed in unison.

Guilt stole over Holton's round face. "I would have told you before, Morgan, but I couldn't find you. I saw you at the funeral, but that wasn't the appropriate time—"

"What did Frank tell you?" Ben asked.

"That day at lunch, before the fire, Frank was worried about something. He wouldn't say what. But he said if anything unusual happened, I should tell Morgan to talk to Esther, that Esther has something for her." His look was apologetic. "I couldn't find Morgan, and I have no idea who Esther is. I'm sorry. I had another problem on my mind, so I didn't take time to ask the right questions."

"It's okay," she assured him. "I know who Esther is."

He sighed. "That's good. I was afraid I'd let Frank down."

Morgan thanked him, but wondered if Holton had misunderstood her father's request. She'd already met Esther Clark, and her father's elderly neighbor hadn't mentioned any last messages from him.

They'd reached the dead end she'd dreaded.

"I'm counting on you," Ben said to Holton, "to help us keep Frank's formula off the market."

"You've got my vote," he promised.

"So long. We'll see you at the board meeting," Ben said.

At the entrance, Morgan spied a pay phone. "Wait. I'll call Esther and ask what Dad gave her."

The phone book chained to the wall yielded Esther's number, but voice mail answered in Esther's chirpy voice. "I'll be visiting my daughter in Sarasota until Saturday, but leave your name and number and I'll call when I return."

"She's away until day after tomorrow," Morgan told Ben.

"I'll have Mrs. Denny make some inquiries.

Maybe she can find out the daughter's name and number and we can contact Esther there.''

Morgan shrugged, afraid to get her hopes up. "If Dad had left Esther anything important, wouldn't she have told us that night at his condo?"

Ben placed his arm around her shoulder. "Not necessarily. You caught her by surprise."

"Okay, maybe Esther does have something for me from Dad, and she just forgot." Her small ray of hope dimmed. "But whatever it is might have nothing to do with Lashner."

"You're so stressed out, everything looks grim." He tugged her closer and pressed his lips against the top of her head. "For a few hours, let's forget Lashner. After some dinner and a good night's sleep, you'll feel more optimistic. You're tired, that's all."

She yearned to return his embrace, to lose herself in the warmth of his arms, the fire of his kisses. But she didn't dare. Feeling vulnerable and confused, she pushed away.

"You're right," she said. "We'll uncover something to make Lashner pay."

But she didn't really believe it.

"DON'T GET UP," Ben ordered. "I'll take care of these."

He rose from the table in the cottage kitchen and began removing plates and glasses to the sink.

Morgan relaxed and watched him work. The irony of Benjamin J. Wells, CEO of Chemco and multimillionaire, clearing the table and scraping dishes wasn't lost on her, but he approached the task as if he'd done it every day of his life.

In fact, Ben had pampered her from the moment they'd walked in the door. He'd tuned soft music on the radio, guided her into an easy chair and propped her feet on the ottoman. Before covering her with an afghan, he'd removed her shoes and drawn the shades.

Exhausted, she had drifted off to sleep. The living room had been dark when she awoke and wandered to the kitchen to discover the linen-draped table set for dinner with lighted candles and a centerpiece of long-stemmed red roses. As if by magic, but more likely with Harper's and Mrs. Denny's help, Ben had produced a full-course Italian meal.

Throughout dinner, she had experienced the strange sensation of being split in half. One part of her enjoyed the food and conversation, while her other half focused totally on Ben. He had sheltered her, saved her life and now stirred her senses as no man ever had, filling her with longing that affected her like a delicious madness.

Had he guessed how much she wanted him? While part of her discussed favorite movies and tastes in music, another desired him in more ways than she'd ever imagined. Her heightened emotions put a whole new spin on her purpose. In addition to avenging her father, stopping Lashner meant keeping Ben alive.

Outwardly composed, she trembled at the thought of losing him. How could she live without him, without the rugged beauty of his smile, the comfort of his companionship, the excitement of his touch, the thrill of his kisses? And if he intended to make love to her, how could she not give in?

From the heated looks he'd given her through dinner, the deliberate way his hands had brushed hers, and the ticking muscle at the base of his jaw, she gathered his need was as great as her own.

Once he'd removed the dishes and only roses and candles remained on the table, an expectant stillness hovered in the room.

"Morgan." He caressed her with his voice.

She rose to face him in the candlelight, and the intensity of his need burned in his eyes.

He grasped her hands and, with excruciating slowness, glided his fingers over her wrists, up her arms and around her shoulders, as if he were a blind man, taking in the shape of her.

But he wasn't blind. His dark, passion-filled gaze explored her face, holding her spellbound. He dropped his hands to her back and skimmed her waist and hips before cupping her bottom, clutching her against him and claiming her lips. She yielded to him like clay to a potter.

Twining her fingers through his thick hair, she opened her lips to him. He tasted of wine and chocolate and burning need. Through three layers of clothes, her breasts, tense and aching, rubbed against his chest.

In one fluid movement, without breaking their kiss, Ben lifted her, carried her into his bedroom to the double bed and lay beside her. Soft light cast a subdued glow, and the scent of frangipani blossomed on the air. When she pulled her gaze from his, she discovered the source of the perfume. Beneath her, soft petals of fragrant frangipani in white and pink were scattered across the sheets. On the nightstand, a grouping of pillar candles threw shimmering light across the bed.

The profusion of candles and petals, revealing the romantic nature of the commanding and pragmatic man, delighted her.

Ben cradled her face in his hands. "Are you sure this is what you want? If not, I'll stop whenever you say."

She closed her eyes against the passion flaring in his. Was she sure? Without question, her body wanted him. And her heart loved him beyond reason. But her head tormented her with doubts about loving a man who had once deceived her.

The two-thirds majority won.

She opened her eyes and gazed directly into his, experiencing again the sensation of falling forever into their mahogany depths. "This is what I want."

He kicked off his shoes and drew her against the length of him with a low moan of satisfaction. She could feel how much he wanted her as his body pressed against hers. With a deep, shuddering sigh, she pulled back enough to undo his buttons and remove his shirt. She traced the outline of his scars.

"Not a very pretty sight," he murmured in a matter-of-fact, if breathless, voice.

"There's beauty in selflessness and courage." She dropped a light kiss on the puckered skin over his heart. "That's what these remind me of."

With deft fingers, he undressed her, and a wave of giddiness spiraled in her, rising like vapor from a hot street after a midday summer rain. Dazed, she watched him enjoying the sight of her.

"Do you have any idea how unbelievably beau-

tiful you are?'' he said with awe as his fingers
brushed her cheek. ''Your skin is as smooth and soft
as these.''

He scooped pink and white petals in his palms and
rained the fragrant blossoms across her bare flesh.
Lowering his head, he breathed in the sweet scent
and nuzzled her breasts, tracing the edge of one nip-
ple, then the other, with his tongue. As shivering sen-
sations shot through her, she dug her fingers into his
back until the need to be closer overpowered her.
Slipping her hands between them, she unsnapped his
slacks and tugged off his remaining clothes.

The euphoria of lying skin to skin, unhampered by
cloth or modesty, brought back her dizziness with a
vengeance, and when he slid his fingers between her
legs, agonizing pleasure detonated through every cell
of her body.

When she gasped with delight, he nibbled her ear.
''That's only the beginning.''

Although the length of their bodies joined, she
longed for him inside her. ''Now,'' she begged.

He kissed her again, deeply, positioning himself
above her and gently parting her thighs.

When he entered her, her heart leaped, faltered,
then matched the pulsing beat of his movements. He
drove her higher and higher until her entire body was
inflamed by the feel of him, by his voice calling her
name and the stark and sensuous pleasure mirrored
on his face.

Instinctively, she angled her hips toward him,
awed at how perfectly their bodies conformed, as if
in some distant, primeval past, they had been one,

then broken, and now at last were fused to their original state.

His gaze never left hers as she whirled into dizzying heights, battered by responses that flung her weightless, timeless, over the edge of reality into star-studded space, where nothing existed but the two of them. His cry at climax, ringing in her ears, was her last conscious thought as she yielded to pure sensation.

Back to earth, she nestled, sated but weak, in the crook of his arm. His even breathing fanned her ear, and for the first time in her life, she felt complete.

He propped on one elbow, regarding her with half-closed lids while his hand traced lazy circles on her breast. A lock of dark hair fell across his forehead, and the handsome lines of the face she'd come to love transformed into a smile filled with promise.

Before she could voice her love, he reached for her again. "I told you this was only the beginning."

Talk could wait.

She rolled willingly into his arms.

Chapter Twelve

Ben turned the Chevy off the highway onto a sandy road overgrown with wild grasses and littered with pinecones from the overhanging trees. After a few hundred feet, out of sight of the main road, he eased the car behind a stand of palmettos and shut off the engine.

Beside him, Morgan peered through the windshield into the deepening twilight. "Is it far?"

"Less than half a mile, but we'll wait until dark before making our move."

"Right." Despite her jeans and dark jacket, she shivered.

"Cold?" He gathered her in his arms and rubbed her icy hands.

Snuggling against him, she shook her head. "Scared."

He tightened his embrace. Making love to her last night, sleeping with her body nestled in the curve of his, awakening to more lovemaking, a shared shower and a lazy breakfast had provided a small island of contentment in the frenzied nightmare of the last few weeks.

Their reprieve had been all too brief.

After breakfast, they had planned a daring and dangerous scheme, a last-ditch effort to stop Lashner before he could sell the flawed gasoline substitute.

They'd sat in the cottage living room, and Morgan, her lips still swollen from his kisses, had confronted him. "I want Lashner to pay for killing my father, but…"

Mistaking her hesitation for despair, he had ached with love for her. "You've been through too much. Give me a few hours and I can arrange for a false passport and put you on a flight to Europe or—"

"No." Pressing her fingers against his lips, she silenced him. "I'm not leaving you. Let me finish what I started to say."

From beside him on the sofa, he tugged her onto his lap. "I'm listening."

"Dad is dead. Nothing we do to Lashner can bring him back." She regarded him with somber eyes. "I want to make sure Lashner doesn't sell Dad's formula and cause the death of someone else's father or husband or child."

"Discrediting the formula has been part of our plan all along," he said.

"But it's come a distant third, after staying alive and convicting Lashner of my father's death. We have to rearrange our priorities." Conviction brightened her eyes and reddened her cheeks. "We have to find proof of the formula's flaws *before* the meeting to insure that the board kills the sale."

Pride mingled with his love for her. For someone who dreaded taking risks, she displayed remarkable courage. Her bravery lay not in lack of fear but in her willingness to persist in spite of it.

"I talked with the independent labs yesterday," he said. "They all need more time to prepare reports with credible conclusions on the formula."

"How much more time?"

"You mustn't worry. Even if results aren't available until after the board sells the formula, the facts will eventually cast doubt and stop production."

She shook her head. "We can't wait until after the board sells the formula."

He'd had the same notion but wanted to hear her reasons. "Why not?"

"Because if your board sells a dangerous formula, Chemco will be ruined. You've worked all your life building that company, and my father shared your hopes and visions for it." She lifted her chin and eyed him with steely resolve. "Lashner is determined to kill us, but it's time to stop worrying about ourselves. We should be seeking proof of the formula's defects for the board, even if we die trying."

Had she read his mind? Since encountering Lashner at the country club yesterday, Ben had been planning to search Lashner's house for just such proof. But *not* with Morgan. His plan was risky at best.

At worst, fatal.

"Lashner has armed guards, watchdogs." He clasped her shoulders. "I can't allow—"

"I make my own decisions." She broke from his grasp, sprang off his lap and faced him, arms crossed defiantly across her breasts, her faced flushed with resolve. "If I choose to risk my life breaking into Lashner's house, who are you to stop me?"

Your husband.

The words died in his throat. Although they were legally married and had consummated that contract by making love until the early hours of the morning, once she no longer needed his protection, would she want to remain his wife?

Only time could answer that question.

He drew her closer in the cold interior of the Chevy. Without success, he had tried to convince her he should search Lashner's house alone. Now all he could do was guard her with his life.

In the car, they waited for darkness to cover their approach to Lashner's sprawling Spanish-style mansion in its wooded setting on the edge of the golf course.

"It's almost time," he said.

She pulled out of his arms, withdrew a jar of black greasepaint from a small bag and scooped out a dollop before passing it to him. They smeared their faces and the back of their hands with the light-absorbing salve, then climbed out of the car.

He turned her toward him in the darkness. "If anything goes wrong, run to the nearest house and call the police."

"Okay," she said, "but shouldn't we alert Detective Paxton beforehand?"

"And make him a party to an illegal search so he can't use anything we find in court?" Ben checked the reassuring bulge of the gun tucked in his waistband at the small of his back. "We're on our own until we find evidence for Lashner's arrest."

"Ben?" Her fingers grazed his cheek in a whisper of a caress. "You'll be careful?"

"We'll both be careful, just as we planned." Only a maximum of self-restraint kept his dangerous desire under control. He brushed her lips in a fleeting kiss that tasted of greasepaint and her own unique sweetness. "Walk behind me. It's rough-going until we reach the golf course."

Breaking a path through the undergrowth, he trudged through the trees with Morgan on his heels. The rustle of pine boughs, the crackle of palmetto fronds and the occasional snap of a twig marked their passing.

After fifteen long minutes, they reached the edge of the fairway. Bending low, they raced across the well-tended green of the fifth hole to the thick shrubbery at the back of Lashner's estate. Lights blazed from tall windows at the rear of the house and illuminated large rectangular patches of the lawn.

With satisfaction, Ben surveyed the weakest link in Lashner's security, his partner's illogical refusal to install any barricade that blocked access to the house from the golf course.

Ben fell prone behind a clump of azaleas, and Morgan dived beside him.

"The woods at the front of the house might have hidden our approach better," she whispered.

"He's concentrated his security at the front, with a wall and gate and an armed guard. Back here, all we have to outsmart are—"

Furious barking interrupted him. Lashner's pack of eight Dobermans had heard them, and the ground shook as the dogs advanced.

"Don't panic." He threw his arm around Mor-

gan's shoulders, and they pressed their faces against
the sandy dirt. "Just lie still."

"If they attack, can't you shoot them?"

"If the dogs attack, we're dead, anyway. The
guards will hear the noise and find us. If the dogs
don't kill us, they will."

Holding his breath, he prayed his plan would
work. He had been a frequent visitor to Lashner's
house before his partner's treachery, and the dogs
knew his scent. Morgan was dressed in the jeans he'd
worn that afternoon and one of his old jackets. He
counted on his scent on her clothes, and the packet
of meat scraps in their pockets, to quiet the animals.

If he'd guessed wrong, the dogs would tear them
apart.

Deafened by the Dobermans' clamor, he clutched
Morgan closer as the pack surrounded them. A wet
nose nuzzled the back of his neck, another his ankle,
and a third thrust a nose between the legs of his
jeans. Morgan's muffled cry suggested she'd suffered
the same indignity.

He stiffened, ready to fling himself across her if
the dogs struck, but, one by one, the canines fell
silent, intent first on sniffing, then licking Ben.

They remembered him.

As he slumped with relief, a man's shout at the
dogs from the back of the house shattered the silence.

"Wonder what spooked 'em?" the man said.

"Probably a damned rabbit," a harsher male voice
answered. "But they shut up so quick, they musta
caught it."

"Should we call 'em back?"

"You heard what the boss said. He wants the

mutts on guard until Wells and the lady are out of the way."

A door slammed, and everything was quiet except the dogs' snuffling.

Ben rolled slowly onto his back and burrowed into his jacket pocket for the bag of meat scraps. Beside him, Morgan did the same. The Dobermans, pushing and shoving, tails wagging, gulped the treats, then trotted away.

"Ready?" Ben whispered.

"Ready."

Scrambling on hands and knees, they reached the back of the house and hid behind the fronds of a low palm. Music and occasional bursts of laughter drifted from the front of the house. Lashner was entertaining again.

"Perfect," he whispered into Morgan's ear. "With all that noise, nobody will hear us. Let's go."

The unlocked back door opened into a mammoth kitchen, which Lashner's efficient staff appeared to have already cleaned after dinner.

Morgan scanned the room and pointed to an interior door. "There."

Under the bright glare of fluorescent lights, Ben gazed at her in astonishment. "How can anyone look so gorgeous in oversized clothes with black gunk all over her face?"

"Stay focused." She grinned and pushed him toward the door.

He cracked it open and peeked into the hallway. The passage was empty.

"Move, fast!" He didn't wait for Morgan. They'd spent hours earlier studying the detailed floor plan he'd sketched. She knew they were headed to Lashner's study at the far end of the corridor.

They bolted down the passageway into the study and closed the door behind them. A small brass lamp with a parchment shade cast a dim circle of light on a massive mahogany desk. The rest of the room remained in shadow.

Following their plan, Morgan scurried behind the desk and began searching drawers on the left. Ben explored those on the other side. As they flipped through files and papers, neither spoke.

When Lashner's voice sounded in the hall, they froze.

Morgan quietly closed a drawer and slipped behind a heavy velvet drapery. Ben did the same.

In the pitch darkness behind the thick fabric, he reached for Morgan's hand and strained to hear what was happening.

The study door opened.

"Have a seat," Lashner said in an irritated tone. "I'll pour you a brandy to calm you down."

The other person mumbled an unintelligible reply, and the leather of one of a pair of burgundy wing chairs rustled as someone settled on it.

Glasses clinked on the sideboard, and liquid gurgled and splashed.

"Here," Lashner said impatiently. "Drink this and stop worrying. Everything's under control, I tell you."

His companion replied with a harrumph of disbelief.

"They'll both be dead before dawn," Lashner

said. "It's taken an army of private eyes and a fortune in bribes, but I've found where they're hiding."

Morgan gripped Ben's hand in the darkness. If hearing her own murder discussed surprised her, the calm pressure of her fingers didn't convey her fright.

"Good," the other murmured.

Ben couldn't identify the speaker, not even by gender. He had guessed Lashner might have an accomplice, but had no clue to who the conspirator might be. Remembering Lashner's sudden appearance at the country club, he wondered again if Rhonda Covill was in league with Rob.

Lashner gave a satisfied chuckle. "My men forced Ben's hiding place out of Tom Hendrix's nurse. Threatened to harm her kids if she didn't cooperate."

Shirley Wilder, Tom's nurse, was a young widow, struggling to raise three children on her own. Lashner's men had apparently terrified her. Ben had believed his disgust with Lashner had already reached its limits, but fresh revulsion swelled in him. Only strict self-control kept him from leaping from his hiding place and strangling the man.

"When Ben and Morgan return to their cottage," Lashner continued, "they'll find a surprise waiting for them. Those two will never bother us again."

His guest must have looked skeptical, because Lashner explained, "There'll be no trail leading back to us. My experts will make Ben's death look like complications from his injuries. Morgan will simply disappear from Gulfside. They'll dump her body in another state. Then we'll sell the formula without opposition and reap the profits. All the profits. I'll be out of the country, beyond the reach of the law before they notice the company accounts have been cleaned out. Your share will be deposited in a Swiss bank, and no one will be the wiser.''

Silence fell in the room, and fearing they'd been discovered, Ben held his breath and clamped Morgan's hand tighter until Lashner spoke again.

''I'll miss this house, this country, but I've always wanted to live on the Portuguese coast.'' His ruthless laugh echoed in the room. ''With Chemco's money, I'll live there in style for the rest of my life. Now, let's get back to the party. Being gone too long will undermine our alibi for tonight.''

Noises indicated the visitor had risen. Glasses clinked on the sideboard, and the study door opened and closed. Ben kept pressure on Morgan's hand, holding her until he was convinced the room was empty.

As insurance, he allowed several moments to tick by before he peered around the edge of the drape.

Lashner was gone.

Ben released Morgan, flung the curtain back and returned to the desk. Morgan joined him, and in silence they resumed their search.

Tension, heightened by the danger of imminent discovery, intensified in the room. Papers rustled as he and Morgan skimmed through folders, replaced them and picked up others. Morgan's sudden gasp of surprise announced her discovery, and her blue eyes glowed with excitement when she passed him a thick accordion folder.

Ben scanned the file's contents, a bound book of formulas and memos, plus several loose pages, then tucked the file into the waist of his jeans and zipped his jacket over it. "We've found what we came for. Let's go."

Their previous luck held as they exited the house and crossed the lawn without an uproar from the dogs or an encounter with the guards. After crossing the fairway at a run, they plunged into the woods. Ten minutes later in the Chevy's dark interior, they caught their breath.

When his panting eased, Ben started the engine and entered the highway.

"We can't go back to the cottage," Morgan said, "not with Lashner's men waiting for us."

"I know a place to regroup."

"Good." She raised no questions, displayed no wariness.

At other times, he'd witnessed a glimmer of distrust in her eyes, and he didn't blame her. Pretending to be Josh, he'd deceived and embarrassed her. She'd probably require a long time before trusting him completely.

But time didn't matter. After all, they had the rest of their lives together.

Which wouldn't be long, if Lashner's men found them.

Maybe they could nail Lashner first. He smiled, remembering the file beneath his jacket.

"Is something funny?" Morgan asked.

He glanced at her, and the headlights of a passing car illuminated the whites of her eyes. "We're going to make quite a scene, walking into William Holton's hidey-hole, looking like a SWAT team."

She pressed her fingers to her cheeks. They came

away black with greasepaint. "I forgot all about this."

"There's a box of tissues in the glove compartment. What they don't remove, we can wash off. As I remember, the bar's rest rooms aren't far from the entrance."

She retrieved the tissues and cleaned her face. Then she scooted closer and wiped his cheeks with fresh tissues. Her breath warmed his face and her breast brushed his arm, reviving memories of their lovemaking.

Out of nowhere, fear clutched his heart like a fist. She trusted him to keep her safe, but could he? Dumb question. He had no choice. He couldn't live with himself if he didn't.

He turned into an almost-empty parking lot at the riverside bar and parked in the shadows at the rear.

Later, with faces washed and twigs and leaves combed from their hair, Ben and Morgan sat at a booth. Her cheeks glowed where she had scrubbed away the greasepaint, reminding him of how she'd looked last night, flushed and sated against his pillow.

He forced the distracting thought away, ordered coffee from the waitress and placed the folder from Lashner's desk on the table. Morgan opened it, pushed back the sleeves of his too-large jacket and began to read, handing him each page as she finished.

At first, observing her, he couldn't concentrate. His clothes swam on her, but she didn't seem to notice. Other women would have complained about appearing in public in such a get-up, but not Morgan.

Her remarkable self-possession gave her such dignity that few would notice her choice of clothes.

He turned his attention to the papers and began to read.

When she finished the last page, she leaned toward him, excitement glittering in her eyes. "Everything's here, including Dad's memos on the formula's flaws and his refusal to lie at Lashner's request. They're proof of Lashner's motive for murdering Dad."

Ben pointed to several reports from a private investigator. "Looks like Lashner dug up personal dirt on Rhonda Covill and William Holton. He probably intends to blackmail them into voting his way."

"Their votes and his give him a majority. What about Terrence Appel?"

Ben shrugged. "Either Appel was clean, or Lashner hasn't received a report on him yet."

"Or he's already sure of Appel's vote. But the votes aren't important now. Not if we can put Lashner behind bars." Morgan heaved a sigh. "Think of the time we've wasted. If we'd searched Lashner's study two weeks ago, we'd have saved ourselves a lot of trouble."

Bending closer until his face was inches from hers, Ben scowled. "Raiding Lashner's house was an act of desperation. Luck is the *only* reason we got out alive."

Her delectable mouth settled in a stubborn line. "If we'd done it sooner, we could have been lucky then."

"No." Ben cupped her cheek and eased the tension of her lips with his thumb. "We escaped tonight only because Lashner assigned the extra men who usually guard his house to wait for us at the cottage. Without that break, we wouldn't be sitting here now.''

She relaxed and smiled. ''A lucky break that was long overdue.''

Ben's spirits lifted. Their long struggle was almost at an end. He collected the pages scattered on the table and stuffed them into the folder.

''We should take this straight to Detective Paxton,'' Morgan said.

''Right. And as soon as Lashner is locked away, you and I are going to celebrate.''

Her eyes sparkled in the dim light. ''That's the best offer I've had all day.''

''There's one other thing.'' He placed his hand over hers. ''Before I sat down, I called Mrs. Denny from the pay phone. She contacted Esther Clark earlier today.''

''Did Esther say what Dad left for me?''

He nodded. ''The poor old woman was horrified she'd forgotten to give you Frank's latest journal. She insisted on returning home, so you can pick it up tonight.''

Morgan nodded with satisfaction. ''We can stop there on our way to the police. If the journal incriminates Lashner further, we'll take it to Paxton with the file.''

''Paxton can arrest Lashner and his thugs,'' he said, ''and we can get back to our lives.''

At his last words, a familiar wariness etched Morgan's features. Ben longed to discuss their future, to clear away doubts, but there wasn't time. They had to move before Lashner's men realized their prey wasn't returning to the cottage and came searching for them.

THEY NEARED the condominium, and Ben checked the rearview mirror, then relaxed. They were almost home free. No one had followed from the bar or fallen in behind during the thirty-minute ride. Soon Morgan would have Frank's journal, and the police station was only ten minutes away.

He slowed to turn into the condo entrance.

Headlights flashed suddenly, blinding him, as a car speeded toward him, head-on. Morgan screamed and Ben slammed on the brakes.

From a side street, more headlights flared as another vehicle accelerated into the street and rammed Morgan's side of the car.

With the glaring lights obstructing his vision and his breathing jolted by the collision, Ben heard the passenger door open and Morgan's exclamation of defiance. He was fumbling blindly for his gun when someone jerked open the driver's door and pulled him out.

Before he could raise his weapon in self-defense, a blow to the back of his head drove him to his knees. Darkness closed in, and he fought unconsciousness.

"Ben!" Morgan's desperate cry pierced the fog descending on his mind.

Shots blasted, and Morgan's cries ceased abruptly.

Unable to ward off the blackness, Ben slumped to the pavement. Resistance no longer mattered.

Morgan was dead.

Chapter Thirteen

Morgan's ears rang from the blow across her face.

"That'll teach you to kick me," the bald-headed thug muttered in a gravelly voice. "Don't get me riled, lady. That dumb security guard just shot my friend. One more peep outta you and I'll waste you right now, to hell with orders. You understand?"

She nodded numbly. The unknown man had struck Ben with the butt of his gun. Horrified, she'd watched Ben drop to the pavement. His attacker had toppled when the bullet from the security guard's gun hit him, and the other kidnappers had tossed their companion into the black van and sped away.

The bald-headed man on the back seat beside her had dragged her into the blue Buick, and now they were miles from the condo. She didn't know if Ben was dead or alive.

Knowing tears would irritate her already-surly captors, she choked back a sob.

"Where's the file?" the driver demanded.

She recognized his voice, the man from the airport. "What file?"

The thug beside her wrenched her arm. "Does Wells have it?"

She bit her lip to staunch a cry of pain. "I don't know what you're talking about."

The driver punched numbers and mumbled into a cell phone. When he'd finished, he spoke over his shoulder. "Blindfold her. The boss says take her where we planned."

Without resistance, she allowed the larger man to tie a covering over her eyes. She slumped against the seat and prayed Ben wasn't badly injured.

If only she could go to him. She had to find a way to escape. Ben had come to her rescue so often, she'd used up all her luck and couldn't expect him now. She was on her own.

Tears glided down her cheeks beneath the blindfold. Ben had risked his life for her so many times. How could she ever have doubted his love? Images of his irresistible smile, his broad, muscular chest scarred with honor, the unruly hair that persisted in falling over his broad forehead, the strength of his embrace and the intoxication of his kisses drove away the darkness in her mind.

Unwilling to risk rejection, she hadn't told him she loved him. Only the intensity of that love sustained her now. She had to stay alive, if only to let Ben know how much she cared.

The car phone rang and the driver answered. She listened for some clue to where they were taking her, but the driver said nothing before hanging up.

"Hey, lady," the hated voice called from the front seat. "That was a message for you."

"What?"

"Ben Wells is dead. You might as well tell us where the file is."

Shock robbed her of speech. Ben couldn't be dead. She had to apologize for doubting him, to tell him how much she loved him, how she couldn't live without him....

The cold fact hit her like a speeding train.

She couldn't live without him. But Ben was dead. Lashner's men had killed him.

"Go to hell," she snapped at the driver.

This time when the bald-headed man struck her, she lost consciousness.

BEN GROANED and opened his eyes.

In the distance, the howl of approaching sirens pierced the silence. Hunching over him, Burt, the condo's security guard, eyed him with concern.

"You lie still, Mr. Wells," he said. "The police and paramedics are on the way."

Ben propped himself on his elbows. "Morgan?"

Burt hunkered down beside him. "They took her."

"Was she...hurt?"

"Alive. And kicking." Burt managed a bleak grin. "She won't make things easy for them."

Ben closed his eyes. The guard didn't know how easy killing her would be for Lashner's assassins.

"They tried to take you, too," Burt said, "but I saw what was happening. As soon as I'd called 911, I ran to help. When I shot the guy who beaned you, they took off. Guess they thought you were a goner, passed out like that and white as death."

A police car and unmarked vehicle skidded to a halt, and their blaring sirens stopped midshriek.

Ben accepted a hand from Burt and pulled to his feet. His head swam from the blow, but he couldn't allow dizziness to slow him. He crossed the street to the unmarked car and met Paxton climbing out.

"Lashner's men have Morgan," Ben said. "They plan to kill her and dump her body in another state."

With his rumpled trench coat and tousled hair, Paxton bore an uncanny resemblance to television's Columbo. "You sure you're okay?"

"I won't be if Lashner harms Morgan."

The detective nodded and pulled out a small notebook. "Just answer a few questions first."

"There's no time." Ben choked out the words. "Morgan's as good as dead if we don't find her fast."

Paxton studied him a second, then shoved the notebook back in his pocket. "Hargett," he yelled to the uniformed officer, "take these people's statements. When you have a description of the perps and the vehicles, send out an all-points bulletin."

"Yes, sir," the young patrolman answered.

"I'm coming with you," Ben said to Paxton.

The detective held him back with a meaty hand splayed across his chest. "I can't let you do that. Let the paramedics check you out, then go home. I'll call you when we've found her."

Paxton hopped into his car and picked up the radio mike. Ben heard him calling for backup before he drove away with his siren howling again.

"Mr. Wells?"

Ben pivoted at the unexpected sound of Harper's voice. "What are you doing here?"

"There's an important message for you, sir." The valet nodded toward the limousine parked at the curb.

"In a minute." Ben waved away the approaching paramedic and turned back to Harper. "I have to give Officer Hargett a statement."

And then I intend to follow Paxton.

Harper, his usually stiff expression fierce, shook his head. "No time, sir. It's a matter of life and death."

The valet glanced from Ben to the patrolman and back, then shook his head again. Puzzled at Harper's strange behavior and frustrated at the delay in trailing Paxton to Lashner's, Ben stomped to the limo, climbed inside and slammed the door behind him.

Harper settled behind the wheel, started the engine and drove away.

"What so important?" Ben demanded.

"You have a caller on hold, sir."

Ben grabbed the car phone. "What is it?" he blurted impatiently into the receiver.

"An exchange," Lashner's unctuous voice announced.

Ben's blood boiled. "I'll kill you, you bastard, if you harm Morgan."

"She won't be hurt if you do as you're told," Lashner snapped. "First, you mustn't talk to the police."

"Too late," Ben said with grim pleasure. "They should arrive at your house within seconds."

Evil colored Lashner's chuckle. "They won't find her here. I'm in the middle of a party, remember?"

Ben's heart skipped a beat. "Remember?"

"You can't outsmart me, no matter how hard you try, so you might as well cooperate. I discovered the file missing from my desk not long ago and suspected you had stolen it."

Ben spread his hand across the front of his jacket, and the folder crackled beneath his fingers. His attackers had missed it, and in his concern for Morgan, he had forgotten about it.

"Since the file includes the report from Hendrix's nurse," Lashner said, "I knew you wouldn't return to the cottage or your house, so I set my trap at Frank's condo, the most logical alternative."

"Where's Morgan?"

"I mentioned an exchange. Bring me the file within thirty minutes and I'll set Morgan free."

Morgan's frantic cry echoed in Ben's mind. As long as he held the file, maybe Lashner would keep her alive as negotiating leverage.

"Let me speak to her," Ben said.

Lashner laughed again. "You aren't listening. I told you she isn't here."

They've already killed her, Ben thought, then shoved the unbearable idea away. "How can I be sure you haven't harmed her?"

"You can't," Lashner answered. "But returning my file is your only hope of saving her."

Ben didn't trust Lashner as far as he could spit, but negotiating could buy him time. "I'll need more than thirty minutes to retrieve the file."

"Nice try, but I can't allow you time to copy the file for the police. Thirty minutes."

"At your house?" Ben asked.

"A car will meet you at the gate." A sharp click indicated Lashner had hung up.

Ben had no intention of showing up at Lashner's. Once the file was back in his possession, Lashner would kill him and Morgan. "Harper, pull over."

The limo slowed to a stop. Ben removed the laptop computer from its concealed storage space and connected its modem to the car phone. Within seconds, he had accessed courthouse records and was scanning a list of properties owned by Robert Lashner.

He believed Lashner when he'd said Morgan wasn't at his house. The man knew he was under suspicion and wouldn't jeopardize himself by detaining her where the police might search. His thugs had to be hiding her somewhere else, somewhere isolated and secure.

Ben scrutinized each of Lashner's holdings as it flashed on the screen. All were commercial properties in well-lit, highly traveled areas, unsuited for concealment. Morgan's time was running out.

He called up the final listing.

A citrus grove.

Miles off the main highway, a perfect place to retain a reluctant prisoner. Or commit murder.

He gave Harper directions to the property, and the valet floored the gas pedal.

Ben stowed the computer and reached to the back of his waist. His gun was gone. He'd drawn it during the attack, but had left it in the street when the police arrived. Harper, his bodyguard as well as valet, would have one, hidden in a shoulder holster beneath his dark suit.

Harper was pushing the limo well over eighty, but the miles dragged by. Morgan filled Ben's thoughts. The first day he'd met her, she'd been shaken and bruised from the hit-and-run, grieving for her father, but terribly brave. The memories of her lovely face, angled toward him in the moonlight, the silky smoothness of her skin, the warmth of her lips and the tender fierceness of her lovemaking tortured him with poignant sweetness.

Fear shoved the memories aside and gripped him with a cold iron hand. He was risking Morgan's life on the chance he could read his partner's ruthless mind. If he had guessed wrong, he would lose everything that ever mattered.

The limo rocked on its expensive suspension as Harper left the highway for a sandy track winding through acres of mature citrus trees. Overhanging branches blocked the moonlight and plunged the limo into darkness.

"Kill the headlights, drive off the road and hide the car among the trees," Ben said to Harper. "We'll go the rest of the way on foot."

No sooner had Harper veered between two towering trees than the lights of a car on the track behind them illuminated the limo's interior.

"Do you think they spotted us?" Harper killed the engine, unfastened his seat belt and drew his gun.

"We'll know soon enough."

Ben held his breath and waited.

WHEN MORGAN CAME TO, dampness ate into her bones like acid, and the stench of mildew and decay filled her nostrils. She raised her head and tried without success to peer beneath the blindfold. Shifting her aching body, she realized she was no longer in the car but tied to a hard wooden chair with her hands bound behind her and a foul-tasting gag in her mouth.

She listened, hoping for a sound to identify her surroundings, but silence thundered around her. She dropped her chin to her chest and yielded to the darkness.

Lashner murdered your father, an inner voice goaded her, *and now he's killed Ben. Are you going to sit there and let him get away with it?*

She was helpless. There was nothing she could do.

Don't give up. That's exactly what Lashner wants.

A muffled clunk sounded behind her. Someone was coming. Given the chance, she would fight. If they were going to kill her, anyway, she'd at least go down swinging.

A door squeaked, and she tensed. Floorboards creaked as someone approached, and fingers fumbled with the bonds at her wrists. With her hands free, she crooked her arm and jammed her elbow toward her captor's groin. An iron hand clamped her wrist, blocking the blow, while another ripped the blindfold from her face.

She blinked in the darkness, afraid she'd lost her mind.

Ben crouched beside her, a finger against his lips.

Happiness exploded through her, and she would have thrown her arms around him, but the warning in his half-closed eyes stopped her.

In the next instant, someone loomed behind Ben in the darkness, and she widened her eyes in alarm.

Alerted by her expression, Ben whirled and chopped the guard's wrist with the side of his hand, sending the bald man's gun skittering across the floor into a pitch-black corner.

With lightning quickness for such a big man, the guard lunged. Equally quick, Ben stepped aside and his attacker sprawled headlong, a victim of his own momentum.

The guard's angry curses rang in Morgan's ears. She held her breath, praying Ben, weakened by his injuries, could defeat the powerful, outraged man.

The bald man scurried to his feet, and Ben knocked him down again with a hard blow to the jaw. Unconscious, the guard lay immobile while Ben bound the man's wrists with Morgan's blindfold and recovered the gun in the corner.

He removed her gag, untied her feet and pulled her into his arms. His lips moved against her ear. "We have to wait here until Harper disables the other guard."

She didn't protest. As long as his arms were around her, she'd stay. Forever, if he asked her.

The door of the musty engine house slammed against the wall, and Harper filled the doorway. "The other guard won't be giving you any trouble, sir."

The valet disappeared as quickly as he'd arrived.

Ben held her at arm's length, his eyes burning in the darkness. "It's all over now. Let's go home."

STUMBLING FROM WEARINESS, Morgan entered the living room of Ben's house. Ben and Harper had handed the two captured thugs over to Paxton. With the kidnappers' testimony and the incriminating contents of the file and her father's journal that Officer Hargett had picked up from Esther, the detective had obtained a warrant for Lashner's arrest.

She and Ben had waited at the station for hours until Lashner and his other hirelings had been locked away. During that time, Ben had been polite but subdued. He had brought her coffee and insisted that her bruised cheek and rope-burned wrists were tended. He'd reserved his comments for Paxton.

Once again Ben had saved her life, and now the moment of truth had arrived. When he'd embraced her in the run-down shed, he'd stated, "It's all over." Soon she would learn the meaning of his ambiguous *all* and *it*. Had he referred only to Lashner's murderous scheming or included their marriage in the broad scope of his observation?

Uncertain how to respond, she had said little at the station or during the ride back to Ben's house, afraid to risk making a fool of herself with unrequited declarations of love.

"Mrs. Denny's laid a fire." She nodded toward the embers smoldering behind gleaming brass andirons in the living room fireplace. "I'm too keyed up to sleep. Do you mind if we sit a while before going to bed?"

"Is something wrong?"

Longing to ask the status of their marriage but unable to find the right words, she shrugged. "I was wondering about Rhonda Covill and Terrence Appel and what part they played in Lashner's scheme."

Ben sank onto the sofa before the fireplace and

tugged her next to him. "Rhonda turned over Lashner's blackmail letters to the police. Lashner had threatened to reveal her affair with the tennis pro to her husband if she didn't vote to sell the formula. She swears she had no part in your father's death."

"Do you believe her?"

"She and Frank were friends. I don't think even blackmail would have forced her to harm him."

"What about Appel?" Morgan asked, still avoiding the topic of their marriage.

"Paxton sent officers to his house to bring him in for questioning. We can't be certain Appel was the person in Lashner's study, but he was the only board member without a blackmail report in Lashner's file."

He circled her with his arm. She rested her head on his shoulder, wishing she could stay there forever, and gathered up her courage. The status of their relationship had to be determined. She had to know if their marriage was over. "It's not Appel I'm worried about."

"You should be," a voice boomed behind them.

Ben leaped to his feet, and Morgan jumped up beside him. Terrence Appel, his eyes glittering with a strange light, stood in the doorway, holding a large glass vial of clear liquid in front of him.

"How did you get in?" Ben demanded.

Appel smiled. "I charmed Mrs. Denny before you arrived. Told her I had important information on the murder of Frank Winters. She opened the gate, then the front door, and said I could wait for you."

"Where is she?" Morgan asked. "You didn't hurt her?"

"She's in the kitchen, trussed up like a chicken," Appel said, "but all right. For now."

Waving the glass vial, he walked toward them.

Ben, amazingly relaxed, advanced to meet him. "What's this all about, Terrence?"

"If Rob's plan had worked, I'd be a powerful and wealthy man," Appel said.

"You're already powerful and wealthy," Ben said in a reasonable voice.

Appel shook his head. "It wasn't enough."

Morgan noted the desperation in the man's eyes. Ben had told her Appel was a multimillionaire. His crazed desire for more money made no sense.

Appel must have seen the puzzlement on her face. "I'm a self-made man," he explained. "Raised myself from poverty and nothingness by my own bootstraps."

"You should be proud of your accomplishments," Ben said. "Don't throw away all you've worked so hard for."

Appel's bitter laugh crackled in the stillness. "I already have. Bad investments. Gambling debts. The money from the sale of that formula was my only hope."

"There's always hope," Morgan said softly, trying to calm the man's agitation.

His thatch of thick white hair fell into his eyes as he shook his head. "Not if I'm dead. Without the money to pay back my debts, I'll be killed by the sharks who covered my gambling obligations. That money was my only chance to stay alive, and now you two have ruined everything."

"Have a seat," Ben said. "I'll fix you a drink and

we'll see what we can work out. I can loan you the money to pay off your tab.''

Morgan wondered why Ben kept talking until she realized he was stalling, waiting for Harper to return from the garage. Together he and Harper could over-power the older but athletic man. Ben had dispatched her bald abductor with ease, but the effort had taxed him, evidenced by the strain on his face and the al-most imperceptible flinch when he moved his right arm.

Appel held his ground. ''I have my pride. I'd rather die than take charity from you. Everything I've worked for all my life will be gone. Now that Rob Lashner's been arrested, he'll spill the facts about my involvement, just to ease his own punishment. My reputation will be ruined. Even if I don't go to prison for the rest of my life, I'll be back where I started fifty years ago. A penniless nobody.''

Morgan's anger boiled over. ''At least you're alive. That's more than I can say for my father.''

''All life is fleeting.'' Appel glanced at his watch. ''And ours will be over in just a few minutes.''

''I wouldn't be so sure,'' Ben said easily.

''Don't count on Harper.'' Appel lifted his eye-brows in a patronizing smirk. ''I knocked him out cold before coming back into the house.''

Without Harper's assistance, Ben was too ex-hausted to handle Appel on his own. Morgan would have to help, but Appel was too strong for her to attack without a weapon. She eased toward the fire-place with her hands behind her back and grasped the handle of the brass poker.

''You've always been a straight shooter,'' Ben

was saying to Appel. "How did you get embroiled in gambling debts?"

"You couldn't understand," Appel said with a sneer, "how humiliating it is to bow and scrape before a chairman of the board who's a boy half your age. Your immature ideas cost me millions. Too many times you vetoed lucrative projects over my objections. I'd hoped my gambling wins would recoup what my rejected projects would have brought in."

Ben displayed no reaction to the specious insults. "Sit down and let's talk this out. More violence isn't the answer."

Appel threw back his head and issued a high-pitched laugh that raised the hair on Morgan's neck. "You can't talk your way out of this, my glib-tongued friend. My life is over. I have nothing left but revenge."

Ben stepped toward him.

"Stay back," Appel shouted. "When I'm ready, I'll toss this vial into the fire. An appropriate ending for us all, don't you think, blown to bits by Frank's formula that started this whole mess?"

"At least let Morgan go. She's done nothing to you." Ben spoke to Appel, but his eyes met hers unflinchingly. The intensity of the love reflected in their brown depths filled her with an incredible peacefulness, in spite of her fear.

Determined that Appel would not steal their chance for happiness, she gripped the poker firmly and, pretending to head for the door, sidled closer to the old man.

"She hasn't done anything—except help destroy

my plans." Appel glared at her, and she stopped.
"She stays here and dies with us."

Appel stood about eight feet from the fireplace,
Morgan within a few feet of him, and Ben remained
close to the hearth, where he could see the poker she
clasped behind her, hidden from Appel's view. She
glanced at Ben, who bent his head in an almost indiscernible nod.

Appel detected Ben's gesture. "Scheming won't
help you now."

He lifted the vial and cocked his arm. Morgan
twirled the poker from behind her back and slashed
it across Appel's wrist.

Too late.

He had released the vial.

As if in slow motion, the glass cylinder turned end
over end, tumbling in an unerring arc toward the
burning embers, enough gasoline substitute to level
half the house in the resulting explosion.

From the corner of her eye, Morgan saw Ben flex
his knees and, with a tightening of his powerful
thighs, lunge in front of the hearth, arms extended.

He landed on his stomach. The vial careered off
his open hands and bounced toward the fireplace.
Whipping onto his back, he thrust his right hand
across the hearth, seized the vial and snatched it
away, just inches before it could shatter in the fire.

Weapon at the ready, Morgan guarded the cringing
Appel, who cradled his broken wrist against his chest
and whimpered. Ben hoisted himself to his feet and
placed the vial gently on the coffee table.

"Unlike you, Terrence—" Ben lifted his gaze to

hers "—I'm not ready to die. I have too much to live for."

"Me, too." Morgan returned Ben's tender glance with a wholehearted smile, handed him the poker and picked up the phone to call the police.

PREDAWN LIGHT illuminated the gulf. Ben stretched his arms above his head and inhaled the salty tang of the breeze blowing through the open living room windows.

The police had left, taking Appel with them. Ben had showered, but he couldn't sleep. He had dressed in jeans and a sweater and returned to the living room. The house was strangely quiet. For the first time since the fire that killed Frank, an enormous weight had lifted from Ben's shoulders and his spirit.

Footsteps sounded on the terra-cotta tiles of the foyer, and he turned as Morgan entered the room. If he lived to be three hundred, he would never tire of looking at her. Even with her bruised cheek and violet shadows of fatigue beneath her eyes, she was the most beautiful woman in the world.

Her tousled mass of golden hair framed the perfection of her oval face, her blue eyes sparkled with a zest for living, and her smooth, supple lips curved in a seductive smile. She had exchanged her rumpled, oversized clothes for a sapphire velour robe, belted at the waist, that paradoxically highlighted her feminine curves while covering them from head-to-toe.

"Mrs. Denny is settled," she said. "She should sleep for hours. I gave her the tranquilizer Dr. Hendrix prescribed with a cup of herb tea."

"Good," he said with a nod. "Tom took Harper

to the hospital. Even though his concussion is mild, Tom wants to keep him under observation for twenty-four hours.''

"That means we have the house to ourselves," she said in a breathless voice.

"And about time, too." His mind overflowed with images of making slow, languorous love to her in every room.

She flushed, as if reading his thoughts. "Before he left this morning, did Paxton say what was in the journal my father gave Esther?"

Ben nodded. "Frank wrote you a long letter. Part of it instructs you to take it to the police. He outlines his conflict with Lashner over the formula and gives dates and times of every threat Lashner made."

Her eyes blurred with tears. "And the other part?"

"It's personal, but Paxton had to read it, in case there was more about Lashner. Your father expressed his wish that you'd find a good man to marry and have children who'd make you as happy and proud as you made him."

A single tear flowed down her cheek. "May I have the journal back?"

"After the trial." He folded her in his arms.

She exhaled a heavy sigh. "Then everything will be finished."

He drew back and lifted her chin until their gazes met. "Lashner will be finished, but you and I? We're only beginning."

A lump formed in his throat at the love that flared in her face before she closed her eyes and raised her lips toward his. Postponing his longing, he released her and stepped away.

"There's something I've been wanting to do for weeks." He kept his voice matter-of-fact.

"Oh." Disappointment flickered across her face before she turned toward the door. "Then I'll leave you to it."

He caught her hand and tugged her back, crushing her against his chest. "Don't go. I'll need your help."

She snuggled against him. "What should I do?"

"Nothing, for now." He lifted her in his arms. "I want to carry my wife to bed."

"Your wife? I am, aren't I?" She clasped her hands behind his neck. "I like the sound of that."

"We've had the wedding. It's time for a honeymoon." He carried her across the living room, into the foyer and onto the wide stairs.

"Stop!" she cried, halfway up.

He halted. "You haven't changed your mind?"

"Not on your life." She caressed the stubble on his chin before skimming her hand over his injured chest. "But shouldn't you rest? What about your wound?"

He beamed her a Gable grin. "Frankly, my dear, I have more important things in mind."

The tugging at the corners of her delectable mouth canceled her solemn expression. "What's more important than your health?"

Love expanded inside him, almost crushing him with its power. "I want to give you something."

She raised one eyebrow. "A gift?"

"For both of us, actually."

"What is it?"

He continued up the stairs. "The children your father wished for you."

She traced his lips with her finger, shooting fireworks through his blood. "I suppose you'll be all right if we take things slow."

"As slow as you like." He stepped through the bedroom door. "We have the rest of our lives."

Epilogue

"Daddy!" Frank's short, pudgy legs pumped as he darted across the lawn toward the terrace.

Ben, who had just come in from work, scooped the two-year-old into his arms. "How's my favorite boy?"

Frank looped his short arms around his father's neck. "Need a hug."

"One hug, coming up." Ben wrapped his arms around the boy and squeezed. Frank giggled with delight.

Morgan laid aside the bestseller she'd been reading to watch her husband and son. Their enthusiastic embrace filled her with the warm glow of contentment.

"Would you like something to drink?" she asked from her lounge chair.

"Don't get up," Ben said. "Mrs. Denny is bringing iced tea."

He slid Frank to the terrace, and the boy ran back to his toys scattered on the back lawn.

"Get up?" Morgan grinned and smoothed the fabric of her maternity top. "I'd need a construction crane to haul me out of here."

He braced his hands on the arms of her chair and leaned down for a lingering kiss that, even after three years of marriage, shot fireworks through her veins.

"You doing okay?" He sank into the chair beside her and accepted a glass of tea from the tray Mrs. Denny offered.

Morgan took her glass and waited until the housekeeper returned inside. "I can't decide whether I feel more like a duck or a dumpling—and still two weeks to go."

Ben smiled. "It'll be nice having a daughter, especially if she takes after her mother."

Morgan set her glass on the table beside her chair and reached for Ben's hand. "You look tired. Bad day?"

"Just busy." He laced his fingers with hers. "Have you heard the news?"

"Frank and I haven't turned on a TV or radio all day. He loves being outdoors. He'd sleep out here if we let him." With a full heart and misty eyes, she gazed at her son. "I wish Dad could see him."

Ben squeezed her fingers. "He'd be very proud. Frank's a great kid. I bust my buttons every time I look at him."

"Was something interesting on the news?"

He cupped his other hand over their joined ones. "Terrence Appel died in his prison cell today. A heart attack."

Her memories of Appel's and Lashner's attempts to kill her and Ben held no terror. Three years of indescribable happiness had not only dulled those fears but blunted the pain of losing her father. "Wasn't his release scheduled for next month?"

Ben nodded. "Ironic, isn't it? The judge showed mercy with Appel's light sentence. Too bad he didn't live long enough to benefit from it."

"Thank God Lashner's verdict was a different story and his army of highly paid lawyers weren't able to overturn his life sentence."

Morgan watched the sun sink through low clouds along the horizon and turn the blue waters of the gulf golden. Her father had died, and she and Ben had almost been killed. But time had proved the old adage that good could come from even the greatest tragedy. She and Ben had found fulfillment in their marriage. And they'd been blessed with little Frank and his soon-to-be-born sister.

She glanced at Ben to find him gazing at her.

"You look like you just won the lottery," he said.

She sighed with contentment. "In some ways, I suppose I have."

"As of today, Chemco, too," he said.

"What?"

"We hit the jackpot." His expression when he spoke of his company was only slightly less proud than the one with which he'd regarded his son. "Your father's formula—"

"No! You haven't sold it?" She bolted upright with amazing swiftness for a woman in her stage of pregnancy.

He leaned closer to brush a curl off her cheek, and excitement sparkled in his eyes. "Our new chemist took your father's notes and used them to modify the formula."

"It works, without the risk?"

"Yes and no. Your father was convinced the formula was too unstable to be used like gasoline. But with a few minor adjustments he'd suggested, it becomes a safe and effective industrial lubricant that will triple Chemco's profits."

No wonder Ben looked pleased. When Lashner and Appel were convicted, Chemco's reputation had been seriously damaged. Ben had worked hard to repair the company's good name and bring up profits. Today his hard work had paid off.

"That's wonderful," she said. "And you deserve all the credit."

Hand in hand they watched the horizon swallow the last sliver of sun while Frank pushed his trucks across the grass in the warm twilight. The clouds turned brilliant tangerine and mango, a salty breeze rustled the fronds of a nearby palm, and the fragrance of honeysuckle sweetened the air.

"What more could we want than what we have this minute?" Ben said, contentedly.

She winced. "Mrs. Denny and Harper."

"Yes," he agreed, misunderstanding, "we're lucky to have them, too."

"Ben, please." She struggled to sit upright and grimaced in pain. "Ask Mrs. Denny to watch Frank and tell Harper to bring the car."

Ben's handsome face paled beneath his tan. "You mean—"

Her contraction subsided, and she giggled at the panic on his face. "Your daughter has managed to make your perfect day complete. She's decided to come early."

Ben scooped her into his arms and carried her into the house, shouting for Mrs. Denny and Harper as he went, little Frank in tow. Morgan snuggled against his chest and nestled her head in the hollow of his neck.

Thank you, Daddy, she thought, *your wishes for me have all come true.*

Coming in August 1997!

THE BETTY NEELS RUBY COLLECTION

August 1997—Stars Through the Mist
September 1997—The Doubtful Marriage
October 1997—The End of the Rainbow
November 1997—Three for a Wedding
December 1997—Roses for Christmas
January 1998—The Hasty Marriage

This August start assembling the
Betty Neels Ruby Collection. Six of the
most requested and best-loved titles have
been especially chosen for this collection.
From August 1997 until January 1998,
one title per month will be available to avid
fans. Spot the collection by the lush ruby red
cover with the gold Collector's Edition banner
and your favorite author's name—Betty Neels!

Available in August at your favorite retail outlet.

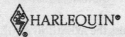
HARLEQUIN®

HARLEQUIN®

INTRIGUE®

A woman alone—
What can she do…?
Whom can she trust…?
Where can she run…?
Straight into the arms of

HER PROTECTOR

By popular demand we bring you the exciting reprise of the women-in-jeopardy theme you loved. Don't miss

#430 *THE SECOND MRS. MALONE*
by Amanda Stevens (August)

#433 *STORM WARNINGS*
by Judi Lind (September)

#438 *LITTLE GIRL LOST*
by Adrianne Lee (October)

When danger lurks around every corner, there's only one place you're safe…in the strong, sheltering arms of the man who loves you.

**Look for all the books in the
HER PROTECTOR miniseries!**

HPT

COMING NEXT MONTH

#437 FATHER AND CHILD by Rebecca York

43 Light St.

Zeke Chambers needed a wife in 24 hours. But could he ask Elizabeth Egan, the woman he secretly loved, to marry him for a pretense, to put her life in danger? But Zeke had no choice: He had to save the life of the child he just found out he had.

#438 LITTLE GIRL LOST by Adrianne Lee

Her Protector

After a fiery crash five years ago, Jane Dolan and her infant daughter were given a new beginning and new memories. So how could she believe reporter Chad Ryker's claims that her family is in hiding and that her precious daughter isn't her child?

#439 BEFORE THE FALL by Patricia Rosemoor

Seven Sins

Wrongly indicted, Angela Dragon is out to find who framed her—even if that means confronting the mob…and escaping a dimple-flashing bounty hunter. Mitch Kaminsky has problems of his own: When Angela learns the truth, will she still want him, or will pride keep them apart?

#440 ANGEL WITH AN ATTITUDE by Carly Bishop

Avenging Angels

To mother an orphaned baby, Angelo's one true love Isobel had turned mortal. Now with a killer on her trail, Isobel needed protection, and Angelo could trust no one with her life. He'd let her down once before; he wasn't about to lose sight of her again.

AVAILABLE THIS MONTH:

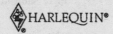